BOYS THAT BITE

MARI MANCUSI

BERKLEY JAM, NEW YORK

THE BERKLEY PUBLISHING GROUP
Published by the Penguin Group
Penguin Group (USA) Inc.
375 Hudson Street, New York, New York 10014, USA
Penguin Group (Canada), 90 Eglinton Avenue, Suite 700, Toronto, Ontario M4P 2Y3, Canada
(a division of Pearson Penguin Canada Inc.)
Penguin Books Ltd., 80 Strand, London WC2R 0RL, England
Penguin Group (Ireland), 25 St. Stephen's Green, Dublin 2, Ireland (a division of Penguin Books Ltd.)
Penguin Group (Australia), 250 Camberwell Road, Camberwell, Victoria 3124, Australia
(a division of Pearson Australia Group Pty. Ltd.)
Penguin Books India Pvt. Ltd., 11 Community Centre, Panchsheel Park, New Delhi—110 017, India
Penguin Books (NZ), 67 Apollo Drive, Rosedale, North Shore 0632, New Zealand
(a division of Pearson New Zealand Ltd.)
Penguin Books (South Africa) (Pty.) Ltd., 24 Sturdee Avenue, Rosebank, Johannesburg 2196,
South Africa

Penguin Books Ltd., Registered Offices: 80 Strand, London WC2R 0RL, England

PRINTING HISTORY
Berkley JAM trade paperback edition / April 2006

Library of Congress Cataloging-in-Publication Data

Mancusi, Marianne.
  Boys that bite / Marianne Mancusi.
    p. cm.
  Summary: Bitten by a vampire after being mistaken for her Goth twin sister, Rayne, sixteen-year-old Sunny is in a race against time as she tries to prevent herself from becoming a vampire permanently.
  ISBN 978-0-425-20942-4
  [1. Vampires—Fiction. 2. Goth culture (Subculture)—Fiction. 3. Twins—Fiction. 4. Sisters—Fiction. 5. High schools—Fiction. 6. Schools—Fiction. 7. Single-parent families—Fiction.] I. Title.

PZ7.M312178Bo 2006
[Fic]—dc22

                                                                        2005055850

PRINTED IN THE UNITED STATES OF AMERICA

15   14   13   12   11   10   9   8

*To all those who stepped in to help
when my house burned to the ground.
I couldn't have rebuilt without you.*

And to Melvin and the FOMs—MMBWY ☺

Acknowledgments

Thanks to Nadia Cornier for agenting this book and to Susan McCarty for buying and editing it. To Paige Wheeler for being a wonderful agent and friend. Thanks for always believing in me.

Thanks to Hank—a fabulous author in her own right. And to Mary, our beloved Activity Director, who has an uncanny ability to talk me down off the ledge. And to Marley for excellent critiquing—as always.

Thanks to The Literary Chicks (Alesia, Lani, and Michelle) for holding the fire auction for me and to Gemma Halliday for all her work setting up the auctions. Thanks to all the agents, editors, and authors who donated critiques and books. The RWA community is amazing!

Thanks to all my old friends at "Rave" in Nashua, NH—the original Club Fang. To Gretchen—who first taught me the allure of vampires. To my parents, who didn't complain too much when I started dressing all in black, wishing I was undead. To Suzanne, for holding "Buffy Night" every Tuesday. And to Joss for creating Buffy in the first place. (You are my hero!)

And finally, thanks to the WoW guild members of Meiyo Seraph for all those nights of much-needed stress relief. Especially Kel (a.k.a. Ed), who has the admirable ability of being able to discuss my book while simultaneously ganking much horde. :)

Sunshine and Rayne

You know, being bitten by a vampire one week before prom really sucks. On soooo many levels.

Okay, fine. I'm sure it'd be equally sucky at other times of the calendar year as well. Photo day at school, for example. Bad time to sport a two-hole hickey on your neck. Easter would blow too—imagine trying to explain to your mom that you can't attend sunrise service because, well, you're allergic to the sun. And then there's Christmas. Sure, you'd sport a good chance of running into Santa, but could you resist the urge to snack on his jolly old jugular?

Now that I think about it, there just ain't a good time to be bitten by a vampire.

That said, you gotta understand. Three hours, twenty-five

minutes, and thirty-three seconds ago JAKE WILDER asked me to prom! I mean JAKE WILDER, people! The hottest guy at Oakridge High School. The heartthrob leading man in every school play with soulful, deep brown eyes and drool-worthy bod. Every girl I know is officially In Love with him—even Mary Markson and she's practically married to her boyfriend, Nick.

But, I ask you, who did the Sex God in question ask to the senior class prom? Uh, yeah, that would be *moi*. Seriously, if you had asked me three hours, twenty-five minutes, and thirty-TWO seconds ago whether Jake Wilder even knew my name, I'd have bet my iPod he hadn't a clue. (And it's a darn good thing I didn't make that bet, 'cause a day without twenty gigs of music at my fingertips is like a day without sunshine.)

That said, I can't tell you what a total and utter bummer it is to be slowly morphing into a vampire one week before the big event.

I'm getting ahead of myself here. Since you don't have a clue as to who I am, you probably don't care all that much about my imminent Creature of the Night transformation. (Mom always says I have the worst manners known to mankind, so I apologize in advance for my shortcomings.)

So okay, all about me for a moment. My name is Sunshine McDonald. Yes, Sunshine, and if you think that's bad, I dread to introduce you to my identical twin sister, Rayne. I know, I know, Sunshine and Rayne—it makes you a little sick to your stomach, doesn't it? Well, you can blame our cruel, ex-hippie parents who (hello!?) grew up in the disco era and should have been hanging out at Studio 54, dancing the night away, instead of at the Harvest Co-Op broiling tofu. But, sadly, no. They preferred peace, love, and stupid baby names to hot dance tunes and bling.

Of course, these days Dad's probably driving around in a hot red sports car while picking up honeys in Vegas. He left Mom to "find himself" about four years ago and has remained lost ever since. We occasionally get guilt-ridden birthday cards with the sincerest apologies and a crisp fifty-dollar bill stuffed inside, but that's about it. I miss him sometimes, but what can you do?

Anyway, back to me. I'm sixteen years old. Five foot four, average weight, dirty blond hair. I've got muddy brown eyes that someday I'm going to hide with blue contacts and a billion annoying freckles that don't fade no matter how much lemon juice I squeeze on them. Mom says I got the freckles from Dad's Irish side of the family. Dad says I got them from Mom's Scottish ancestors. In any case, Rayne and I were cursed in the womb by the bad gene fairy and can't do anything about it.

At school I do okay—an A/B student usually. I like English. Abhor Math. Want to be a journalist when I "grow up." I play varsity field hockey and have twice tried out for the school play, mostly to be up close and personal with Jake Wilder. I have now twice ended up as Heather Miller's understudy and the stupid girl is never sick. I'm talking winning-the-perfect-attendance-award-two-years-running never sick. To add insult to injury, she also has big boobs and throws herself at Jake on a daily basis.

But anyway, I'm sure you're much more interested in the whole vampire thing than Heather Miller's chest. (Though you should see it—she looks like freaking Pamela Anderson!) Basically, the trouble all started when Rayne decided to drag me to a Goth club.

Now for the record, I'm so not into Goth music or that whole scene AT ALL. Not that I'm a Britney lover, of course. I guess you could consider me a John Mayer type of girl. But Rayne, on the other hand, is a full-fledged Goth chick. If I ever saw her wear anything but the color black, I would seriously fall over in shock and awe. She listens to all this bizarre music that you'd never hear on the radio and loves dark, twisted movies that make absolutely no sense. For example, she's seen *Donnie Darko* fifty times and can quote seventeen *Buffy* episodes by heart. When a new Anne Rice book comes out, she camps overnight to be first in line to buy it. (Even though there are plenty of those sicko books to go around, trust me.)

So anyway, two days ago Rayne tells me she saw this flyer at Newbury Comics for an all-ages Goth club up in Nashua, New Hampshire—about twenty minutes from where we live on the Massachusetts border. It's called, if you can believe it, "Club Fang," which has seriously got to be the most cheeseball name on the planet. Rayne, on the other hand, is so excited, I'm half convinced she's going to pee her pants. (Or her long, black skirt, to be exact—the girl wouldn't be caught dead in pants.) And because, as she reminds me, I've known her since birth, it's evidently my twin-sisterly duty to give up any Sunday night plans I might have had to go with her, since all of her friends are too busy.

Lucky me.

1

Goth Me Up—Bay-Bee

"Give me one good reason why I should go tonight."

It's Sunday evening, five P.M., and I'm desperately trying to get out of the big Club Fang outing my sister's got planned for us. I'm not holding out much hope, though. After all, it's a proven fact in life that what Rayne wants, Rayne gets. Period. End of story.

Rayne rolls over from a lounging position on her four-poster bed, props her head up with an elbow, and gives me her best pout.

"Quit your whining. It'll be totally fun and you know it. Besides, I went to see Dave Matthews with you and you can't possibly imagine how painful that was for me to endure. My ears still haven't recovered."

My identical dramaholic rubs her lobes with two fingers, as if they're still causing her pain. Puh-leeze.

"Whatever." I shove her playfully, and she falls back onto the mattress. "As if it's a chore to hear that dreamy voice."

"Chore, no. Cruel and unusual punishment worse than death? Now you're getting warmer." Rayne jumps up from the bed and makes a beeline for her closet. "So you're going. It's decided." She rummages through the hangers, face intent. "Now we need to find you something to wear."

Danger! Danger!

"Oh no you don't!" I cry. "I may be forced to go to this stupid club, but I'm so not undergoing some extreme Goth makeover. There's nothing wrong with what I have on." I stand up and model my tank/jeans/flips combo, which has always served me well.

Rayne turns to look at me for a second—long enough to give me a once-over and roll her eyes—then turns back to her closet. She pulls out a long black skirt and black sweater.

"I'm not wearing a sweater to a nightclub," I protest. "I'll sweat to death!"

"Fine. Jeez. It was just a thought." She crams the outfit back into the overflowing closet, exchanging it for a black (surprise, surprise) tank top. Now while as a rule, I'm totally a tank top type of girl, I tend to stay away from ones made out of vinyl.

"No effing way." I shake my head. "People will think I'm

into S&M and start trying to whip me or handcuff me to the stage or something."

Rayne emits her patented sigh of frustration at my protest, but thankfully returns the bondage outfit to the closet. I, in turn, sit back down on the bed and wonder whether I should be concerned that my twin owns an outfit like that to begin with.

"How about this?" she asks. She pulls out a very cute spaghetti tank with the words *Fashion Victim* written on the front. "It seems rather appropriate."

I throw a pillow at her.

"Only in the most ironic of ways, of course," she amends with a giggle. "Or, there's always this one." She exchanges the tank with another—this one pink with white writing that says *Bite Me!*

"Where'd you get that shirt?" I ask curiously. "It doesn't seem like your type of thing. It's not even black."

She shrugs. "Some vampire let me borrow it a while ago. I keep forgetting to give it back."

"Vampire?" I raise an eyebrow. While I knew Rayne ran with a different crowd, I hadn't realized they fancied themselves creatures of the night. "We're swapping clothes with the undead now?" I guess that would explain all the black.

Rayne snorts. "I just borrowed a T-shirt, smart-ass. But for the record, yes. There's like this whole group of them in

Nashua. They look like Goth kids, but they're really members of an ancient vampire coven."

"You've got to be kidding me," I groan. "Why would anyone want to pretend to be a vampire anyway? Like why is that so cool? Do they go around drinking each other's blood or something?"

Rayne gives me a noncommittal shrug, which tells me she actually thinks it *is* cool, but isn't about to admit it to me. I consider teasing her, but then decide the "live and let live" theory of sisterhood is the best plan of action at this point and drop the subject. After all, I have to hang out with her all night. Having her mad at me is only going to make things that much more painful.

"Okay, I'll wear the *Bite Me* shirt," I say to appease her. At least it's not black. "It'll be my standard response to anyone who tries to hit on me." I giggle. "Someone can come up and be like 'Hey babe, what's your sign?' and I'll just point to my shirt."

Rayne laughs appreciatively and tosses me the tank top. "Of course they might think you're pointing to your boobs in a 'have at 'em, big boy' kind of way."

"Ew!"

"Don't worry," my sister says, swapping her T-shirt for a long, black princess dress ornamented with a ton of lace. Where does she find this stuff? "Most of the boys will be gay, I'm sure. All the good ones are, especially in the Goth scene. You don't get many hetero guys who dig wearing eyeliner."

She snorts. "So, little angelic twin of mine, I'm quite confident that your virtue will remain intact, no matter which T-shirt you wear."

Here she goes again. I knew we couldn't have a whole conversation without Rayne's infamous "Sunny the Innocent" digs. My precious little twin lost her virginity last year and has been bragging about it ever since. You'd think she won an Olympic sex medal or something. But I'm sorry. Meeting some grungy skater dude at camp and sneaking out to do it on the floor of the boathouse is so not my idea of a fulfilling first experience. Call me a girly-girl, but I want my first time to be all candles and roses, not splinters and knee burns. To each her own, I guess.

"So anyway," Rayne continues, taking my silence as license to carry on teasing me, "you can be well assured, your innocence is safe at Club Fang."

I giggle in spite of myself. She sounds like a saleswoman. "Is that printed on the flyer?"

"Absolutely," Rayne declares confidently. "Money-back guarantee."

2

Club Fang

Club Fang turns out to be pretty much what I'd pictured, but mind you I didn't have very lofty expectations for the place. Since it's held in a building that by day serves as a Knights of Columbus hall, there's only so much the promoters can do to Goth it up at night and still be able to tear things down in time for the Veteran's Brunch at six A.M.

Not that they haven't given it the old college try. They've strung flashing multicolored lights in the rafters and hung large white sheets from floor to ceiling, blocking the windows. They set fans behind these sheets so that they billow in the breeze. Slide projectors across the room cast eerie, nondescript images onto the white sheet backgrounds.

In front of the slightly elevated stage area, they've placed the *pièce de résistance*—a bondage cage. At least that's what it's supposed to look like. I think they just took some wire fencing and spray-painted it black.

Behind the "cage," a DJ type with a scruffy beard rummages through records and large speakers pump out overblown Goth, industrial, and electronica sounds. They even have one of those cheesy smoke machines, which totally makes me start coughing the second we enter.

The other club kids don't seem to mind the cheesiness or the smoke. Dressed uniformly in black, they sway to the music, doing a dance that to me resembles getting one's foot stuck in the mud. They slowly, meticulously pull the foot out, only to have the other foot then seemingly get stuck as well, forcing them to repeat the whole process from the beginning.

"School!" Rayne shouts in my ear.

"Huh?" What does she mean, "school"? OMG—does she see someone from our high school? Oh, man, I'd be mortified if someone I knew caught me here in my current ensemble and word got out to my field hockey teammates. I'd never hear the end of it. "Who's here from school?"

"No, I said, 'it's cool!'" Rayne corrects. Oh. Phew. Not that I agreed with her assessment, mind you, but at least it didn't involve me having to hide behind one of those billowing sheets.

"I'm going to get a drink," Rayne says, pointing to a

small, makeshift bar on one wall. Unlike bars in real clubs, of course, this one only serves soda. Too bad. Not that I'm some alky, but in this case a beer might help dull the pain.

"Get me a Red Bull," I tell her. Maybe a megadose of caffeine will be the ticket. Rayne nods and disappears into the fog.

I find a wall and make like a wallflower, wondering why on earth I agreed to this torture. We've been here five minutes and I already have a splitting headache. Not to mention, the stench of the masses makes me want to puke. Seriously, would it hurt to apply a little Secret to your pits before working up a sweat on the dance floor?

I try to give my brain the Pollyanna pep talk.

Okay, try to have a good attitude, Sunny. Rayne has done plenty for you. Stop being so selfish and go with the flow. Who knows, you might even have fun!

Yeah, right. Even Pollyanna-brain doesn't believe that one. Best I will be able to manage is to fake a good time.

"Good evening."

Oh no. A guy. Addressing me. I thought Rayne said everyone was gay here. I look up, ready to point to my tank top, when my gaze falls on the most gorgeous pair of eyes I've ever seen in my sixteen years on the planet. They are literally the color of sapphires. I mean, I've seen plenty of blue eyes in my day, but nothing like these.

Better yet, the eyes are attached to a face equally amazing. I quickly take stock: smooth skin, high cheekbones, sooty black eyelashes. Long brown hair, pulled back in a ponytail. I'm not normally into the long hair thing, but on this guy it totally works. He looks like a blue-eyed Orlando Bloom. (*Pirates of the Caribbean* Orlando, not *LOTR* and certainly not *Troy,* just FYI.) Best of all, unlike the other Gothed-out club kids, he isn't wearing a stitch of black. Just a simple tight white T-shirt and a pair of low-rise jeans. No eyeliner either, thank goodness.

I scan the area, sure that "Orlando" must be speaking to someone other than me. Some supermodel to my right, perhaps. But I see no one in the general vicinity. Hmmm . . .

"H-hi," I say, my words sounding squeaky and young. I hate my voice. Makes me sound like I'm ten. Rayne and I are identical twins and yet she has this sultry, raspy voice somehow. Maybe it's due to her smoking, though, and I'm sorry, but if it's a choice between eventual lung cancer and a squeaky voice, you can call me Minnie Mouse any day of the week.

Instead of replying, the guy reaches out and presses his palm against my cheek. His skin is cool, but his touch scorches my skin. His eyes study my face, then roam my body and I suddenly feel naked under his glare. I give an involuntary shiver and I can feel goose bumps popping up all over my arms. Wow. I can't remember the last time a guy gave me actual goose bumps! Maybe never.

I know I should be questioning why this random guy has approached me in a nightclub and evidently feels it's no big deal to reach out and touch me so intimately, but I can't find the words to voice any objections.

"I'm Magnus," he says in a breathy, dangerous voice with a distinct hint of English accent. "I believe you were expecting me?"

My heart sinks. Damn it, I knew he had the wrong girl. He probably has some blind date he's searching for and mistook me for her. (Though why a guy of his caliber would have to go on a blind date is beyond me. Any date with 20/20 vision would snatch him up at first sight!)

Wait a second here. If he doesn't even recognize his date-to-be, what kind of hold does this chick have on him, anyway? They're obviously not yet a couple, which in my book makes him fair game. I look around, making sure there's no crazy possessive blind date type hovering nearby, ready to claw out my eyes for stepping into her territory. But the coast seems clear.

"Hi, Magnus," I say, having to shout over the music. "I'm Sunny."

He cocks his head, a confused look on his face. Then he touches a finger to his ear and smiles at me. Ah. I get it. He can't hear me over the music. Just when I'm about to retry my intro with a louder voice, he takes my hand and pulls me toward the club's exit.

I can feel my heart pounding in my chest—a billion beats a minute would be an understatement of tempo at this point. Where is he leading me? Should I follow or break away? I scan the room for Rayne—to at least let her know I'll be right back—but she's nowhere to be seen.

We step outside into the crisp night air. It's rather chilly out here, even for New Hampshire in May. The club's bouncer eyes us suspiciously for a moment before turning back to continue flirting with the cute blond jailbait to his right. Magnus leads me down the front steps, still holding my trembling hand in his.

"Uh, where are we going?" I ask, stopping short. After all, no matter how cute this guy is, I know absolutely nothing about him. And logical Jiminy Cricket voices in my head warn of the dangers of following a random stranger out of a nightclub.

He turns and smiles again and my defenses crumble. Surely someone with such a beautiful smile couldn't be dangerous, right?

"It's a bit difficult to hear you in there," he says at last. Wow, I so love his accent! "I thought we could come outside for a little chat."

Okay, a chat. As in a talk. Talking is good. Talking doesn't involve anything Mom wouldn't approve of. Not that I care what Mom would approve of, I remind myself. I mean, I'm sixteen years old—practically an official adult. I've really got to stop the goody-two-shoes routine I've got going on all the time.

"So um, do you come here often?" I ask, trying to make conversation. Too late I realize how clichéd I sound.

He chuckles softly, and I feel my face heat. That's another pain-in-the-butt thing about having light skin and freckles. I blush like nobody's business and there's no hiding it. Hopefully the darkness around us will reduce its fire-engine-red glare.

I want to say more, to redeem myself for my idiotic question, but my tongue just doesn't seem to want to work right. What the hell is wrong with me? My brain says I should be freaking out, but my heart says to go with the flow. After all, how often does a gorgeous guy just walk up to you in a nightclub and start talking? I mean, sure, it may be an everyday occurrence for, say, Paris Hilton, but it so doesn't ever happen to little old me.

We walk behind the building, where there's a parking lot and a single streetlamp casting a yellowish glow on the vehicles. Magnus stops walking and smiles at me. I lean against the building's brick wall and give him a shy smile back.

Now what? I hope he's not expecting some intellectual conversation, because I don't think I can manage it at this very instant.

But verbal discussion seems far from his mind as he takes a step closer, his knee brushing against my inner thigh. The sudden body contact invokes a slightly nauseated feeling in the pit of my stomach. But nauseated in a good way, if that's possible.

He brings a hand to my face again, this time tracing my cheekbone with a smooth finger. His eyes search mine, as if they can see into my very soul. The whole thing is so unnerving and dangerous and sexy, I swear I'm going to fall over and faint.

"You're beautiful," he whispers. "And so innocent."

I frown. God, I hate when people say that. I mean sure, technically I am innocent, Innocent with a capital *I*. But what royally sucks is that it's evidently so easy to tell this about me at first glance. Like, what, am I wearing some big *V* on my chest or something? Rayne is my identical twin and NO ONE ever says SHE looks innocent. Oh, no. The boys think she's all seductive. Kick-ass, even. But never innocent.

"I'm not *that* innocent," I declare, too late realizing that I'm quoting Britney. I really need to keep my mouth shut until I can count on it to say something intelligent, witty, and interesting.

"It's not an insult," he murmurs, his finger drifting to my ear and tracing the lobe. "I find it very, very attractive."

Did I mention how utterly hot he is? And how turned on I am? And how utterly incapable I am of responding to anything he says?

"Oh. Well, um. Thanks. I guess." I laugh my stupid laugh—the one I always break out when I'm nervous. It resembles a donkey's bray and I'm not all that fond of it.

He leans in closer, his mouth so close I can feel his breath on my face. He smells of mint and something spicy I can't identify. "Are you sure you want this?" he asks, searching my face again.

I scrunch my nose, puzzled. Am I sure I want what? This whole encounter really gives me the feeling that I'm missing out on some vital piece of information. By the way he's looking at me, though, I'm getting the feeling he's asking if I'm sure about kissing him. And the answer to that question is *hell yeah*.

"I'm sure," I murmur, hoping my voices sounds husky like Demi Moore's. Like Rayne's. "Very, very sure."

He smiles. "Okay, then. Let's do it."

I close my eyes and next thing I know I can feel his full lips brush against my own. Chills erupt in every crevice of my body and the goose bumps return with a vengeance. Now I'm no kissing expert, mind you (in fact, I'm a bit embarrassed to admit I've only made out with three guys in my entire life), but even I can tell this is an amazing, once-in-a-lifetime kiss. The way his lips press against mine, as if he's starving and hasn't eaten for days. As if he desires something that only my mouth can provide. My lips part, and I can't withhold a soft moan of pleasure. I hope he doesn't think I'm total slut girl for letting him kiss me like this. I mean, I barely know him. But something about this seems so right.

His lips abandon my mouth and kiss a trail down to my neck. I love being kissed on the neck. It is a total turn-on for some reason. The ultralight wisp of his lips brushing against my—

OWWWW! "What the—?" I jump back, horrified.

OMG! Did he just BITE me?

3

The Contract (Signed in Blood)

My hands fly to my neck. I can feel hot blood bubbling from the wound. "What the hell did you do that for, asshole?"

He doesn't even have the decency to look apologetic. Just plants his hands on his hips and frowns. "You said you were sure," he says in a decidedly pissed-off voice. "Damn it, I hate when you kids change your mind at the last minute."

"Sure that I wanted to *kiss* you, not let you munch on my jugular," I retort. "What ever gave you the idea that—" I catch him glancing down at my *Bite Me* tank. Oh. I cross my arms over the writing. "That wasn't meant to be taken literally."

"Look, you knew there was going to be mild discomfort

during the initial procedure. It clearly states that in the contract you signed." Now he looks exasperated.

"Contract? What freaking contract?" This guy is insane. Gorgeous, but clearly and utterly insane.

To my further shock, he reaches into his book bag and pulls out a thick stack of papers, bound with a black binder clip. He holds them up and points to the bottom of page one.

"*Con-tract*," he says slowly, as if addressing a small child.

When did Mister Tall, Dark, and Charming turn into Major Jerk-Off?

"Look, I don't know what you're talking about, but I never signed any—"

He flips to the last page and points to a signature. "*Signature*," he says in the same patronizing tone. I barely resist the urge to slap him. My neck is burning at this point. What did he eat before kissing me, wasabi?

I squint at the signature line, trying to figure out what he's talking about. I gasp as I see my sister's scrawled handwriting at the bottom of the contract.

"What the—?" I whisper. I try to yank the contract from his grasp. He holds on tight—guy's got a killer grip. I look up, staring him down. "What is this?"

He runs a hand through his long brown hair, which has come loose from its ponytail. He looks wild and dangerous and angry. "You know damn well what it is. You went through the class. The testing. You signed your name, for hell's sake!"

"That's not my name, dude. That's my sister's. Now why

don't you tell me what's really going on here?" Oh Lord, what has Rayne gotten herself into now? Some kind of weirdo cult?

Magnus frowns. He glances down at the contract and then up at me. "Your sis—?"

"Magnus?"

I jump a mile as I hear my sister's voice cut across the parking lot. Speak of the devil.

"Oh, Magnus, are you out here? Rosa said you might be out here. I'm ready, you know. Ready and willing, baby," she says, easily mastering that sultry voice thing I was attempting a few minutes before.

I glance over at Magnus, who has suddenly lost his confident swagger and looks like he's sweating bullets. I mean, the guy wasn't all that tanned to begin with, but now he looks positively glow-in-the-dark white. He stares at me, then behind me. I turn around and see Rayne approaching.

"Sunny, what are you doing talking to Magnus?" Rayne asks disapprovingly as she approaches. "He hasn't . . . told you anything weird, has he?"

"Rayne, what the hell is going on here?" I demand.

"There's . . . two . . ." Magnus the once-smooth lover stammers. "But I thought . . ."

"Rayne is my twin sister," I explain to him, marveling at how in control my voice sounds.

"But you look . . . I thought . . ." Magnus trails off.

Rayne's face drains of color. "Oh no," she cries. "You didn't!" She places a hand on my shoulder and yanks me around to face her, peering at my neck. "Oh no!" she cries. "No, no, NO!"

"Will someone please tell me what is going on here?" I demand, hands on my hips. This has gone way too far. "And I mean, now!"

"Now Sunny, don't get mad, but . . ." Rayne begins, her voice trembling.

I shoot her an angry glare. "But WHAT, Rayne?"

"I, uh, think you've accidentally been turned into a vampire."

4

A Bloody Bad Case of Mistaken Identity

"A vampire?" I cry. "Is this your idea of some kind of sick joke?"

Rayne shakes her head. "No joke, Sun. But a serious problem." She turns to Magnus. "How could you have screwed this up? You're supposed to be my sponsor. And you can't even tell when it's not me?"

Magnus moans, then leans over and starts spitting onto the pavement. Attractive. I can't believe five minutes ago I thought he was hot and sexy. Someone I wanted to hook up with. At this point, I'd sooner kiss the Cryptkeeper.

"You look exactly alike," he whines. "How was I supposed to know?" He closes his hand into a fist. "Lucifent is going to kill me."

"Um, technically aren't you already dead?" I ask in my sweetest voice. I'm so over this game already.

He turns around to shoot me an evil-looking glare. "I take it you were absent the day they covered 'figure of speech' in school?"

I raise an eyebrow. "At least I showed up when they taught us not to bite the other kindergarteners."

"Guys, please!" Rayne interrupts. "Stop arguing. This is serious. It doesn't matter why this all happened. Just that it did. And that we've got to make it unhappen. Sunny can't turn into a vampire. She's got field hockey play-offs next week."

For the record, field hockey would be the least of my concerns were I to turn into a vampire for real. I'd be thinking bigger picture: like the fact that the whole "sleeping all day, hunting humans all night" gig might be a deal breaker at all the colleges I'm planing to apply to.

Magnus hocks another loogie on the sidewalk. Ew.

"Uh, do you mind the whole spitting thing?" I ask, backing up to put distance between me and his spray zone. "It's really grossing me out."

He looks up. "I'm trying to remove all traces of your blood from my mouth. You weren't tested first. Who knows what kind of diseases you could be carrying?" he says, a horrified look washing over his face. "You don't have AIDS, do you?"

Of all the . . . Gah! This guy is pissing me off big time. It's not like I freaking asked him to start munching on my jugular. It'd serve him right if I did have some weird communicable disease.

Rayne rolls her eyes. "Puh-leeze. Sunny's pure as the driven snow, Mag. Total Virgin with a capital *V.* So unless she has some hidden heroin addiction she hasn't told me about, I think you're clear. And," she adds with a smirk, "I'm pretty sure she's not a smackhead. After all, she doesn't exactly have that waiflike heroin chic thing going on, now does she?"

"Oh, thanks a lot, Rayne." Now we need to bring up the circumference of my hips as well? This night is getting better and better.

"Right," Magnus says. "No diseases. Well, at least that's something. But still. An unauthorized bite! Do you know how badly Lucifent is going to kill—er, kick my arse? I mean in this day in age no one turns someone into a vampire against their will. It's simply not kosher and an absolute lawsuit waiting to happen."

"I can sue you? Cool." I rummage around in my purse for a pen, wanting to write this down. "Under what? Medical malpractice? Assault with a deadly fang?" I look up. "How much you think the courts would award me for that?"

Rayne frowns. "Sunny, stop being a bitch. Can't you see poor Magnus is freaking out here?"

"*I* need to stop being a bitch? For *Magnus's* sake?" I stare at her, unbelieving. "Uh, hello? He's the guy who walked up and bit me for absolutely no reason whatsoever."

"I had a reason," Magnus remarks, more than a bit sulkily.

"I just thought you were Rayne. A bloody bad case of mistaken identity, that was."

"Look guys," I continue. "I don't know what kind of sick little games you Goth kids like to play, and to tell you the truth, I don't think I want to know. So run along and hang out in graveyards, wish you were dead, whatever floats your little Gothic boat. But I am so out of here." I turn to my sister. "Rayne, find your own way home. I'm no longer in the mood to get down and dirty on the dance floor."

I turn and hightail it for the car. But Rayne comes up behind me and grabs me by the shoulder, whirling me around. Her eyes are wide and fearful and her powdered face is even whiter than normal. (And that's saying something!)

"Sunny, listen to me," she cries. "This isn't a game. Magnus is a vampire. And if he's bitten you, then you're going to become a vampire, too. You've got to take this seriously."

I roll my eyes. "Rayne, sweetie. My dearly deluded twin. I know this may come as a great shock to you, but there are no such things as vampires."

"I used to think that, too. But there are. And Magnus is definitely one of them," Rayne insists. "Mag, show her."

I huff and grudgingly turn around. This oughta be good. "Yeah, Mag, show me."

Magnus lets out a deep, overexaggerated sigh. As if he's weary of the world demanding he prove his creature of the night shtick. I'm sure he gets it a lot.

"Fine," he grumbles, reaching into his bag for a pocket-knife. "Do you want to do the honors?" he asks, flicking the blade open and offering it to me.

"I think I've been honored enough for one day, dude."

"I'll do it. I'll do it," Rayne butts in excitedly.

"What exactly are we doing?" I ask, as Magnus hands the knife over to my eager twin.

"Stabbing him, of course," Rayne says matter-of-factly.

Of course.

As Magnus lifts his shirt to expose his stomach (and his washboard abs, I can't help but notice) I wonder how they've set up this trick. Retractable blade? Blood packet embedded in the tip?

"You know what? I think I'd like to do it after all," I announce. This way I can better figure it out. Then I can denounce them and get on with my night.

Rayne shrugs and hands me the knife. I run my fingertip lightly over the blade. Ouch! A small bubble of blood bursts from the cut. It really is sharp. Hmm.

I hear a soft moan and look up. Magnus is staring at my finger as if I'm a gourmet dessert and he's a *Survivor* castaway who's eaten nothing but rice for the last month. I've never seen such lust in someone's eyes and it's kind of unnerving.

"Do you mind, um, wiping your finger?" he says in a breathy, panicked voice.

"Why, does it bug you?" I ask, waving the finger in question in the air. "Do you want to suck it or something?"

"Sunny, don't tease the vampire," Rayne scolds.

You know, I do have to admit, Magnus has got this vampire act down pat. I think I even see a little drool at the corner of his mouth as he stares, entranced by my bloodied finger, following it with his eyes as a dog would follow a treat.

"Okay, sorry," I say breezily. I slowly bring my finger to my mouth and make a great show of licking the blood away.

Magnus gasps and looks for a moment like he's going to pass out.

"Now that's just mean," Rayne rebukes. "Really, Sunny."

I laugh. They're so serious about all of this. "Okay, okay," I say. "The big bad bloody finger is gone. Let's get back to stabbing."

Magnus, seeming to recover somewhat, lifts up his shirt again. Wow, I wonder how many sit-ups he has to do to attain that kind of bod? Too bad he's such a loser. If he could get a personality transplant or something, he'd be the perfect catch.

I examine the knife again. How does it retract? I don't feel any springs . . .

"Just hurry up and do it," he says. "We don't have all night."

"Right. Wouldn't want you to get caught in the morning sun and get all dusted and stuff," I say with a snort. "Fine.

Here we go." I pull the knife back, then jam it into his stomach as hard as I can.

"Agh!" He screams in pain and buckles over, the knife still sticking out of his abdomen, dark blood seeping from the wound.

"Uh, um . . ." Wow. That looks really real. How'd they get all that blood to come out of the knife? And how does the blade stick in his stomach like that, if it's retractable?

And uh, why is he acting like it really, really hurts for that matter?

"Uh . . ."

I glance over at Rayne, who's watching the scene with cool eyes. What the hell is going on here?

I look back at Magnus. He's fallen to his knees, clutching his stomach, an expression of agony on his face. His hands are almost purple with blood and he's still moaning in pain.

Fear clutches my heart with an icy grip. Did I screw up? Did the blade not retract when it was supposed to?

Did I really just stab a guy in the stomach?

"Are you okay?" I ask worriedly. Dumb question, really. The puddle of blood kind of gives it away.

In response, Magnus falls from his knees to the pavement—in the fetal position, clutching his stomach.

Panicking, I scramble down to my knees and try to turn him over so I can examine the wound. It's positively gushing blood. I'd be totally grossed out if I weren't so scared.

"Oh my God, I think he's really hurt," I shriek, turning to locate my twin. "Rayne! Call 911. He needs an ambulance!"

I turn back to Magnus, searching for a way to stop the bleeding. Should I take the knife out or leave it in? My breath comes in short gasps, along with choking sobs as my life flashes before my eyes.

I, Sunshine McDonald, have just stabbed someone in the stomach. And now he could die. And I'll be responsible. They're going to charge me with murder. Toss me in jail and throw away the key. Do they have the death penalty in New Hampshire? Oh my God. Why did I volunteer to take the knife? What possessed me to stab a deluded teenager who thinks he's a vampire in the stomach? *Stupid, Sunny. Truly stupid.*

Tears streak down my cheeks as I crouch beside Magnus. "Are you okay?" I ask, sobbing. "Can you hear me?" I lean in closer. "Do you see any white light? If so, I'm begging you, do not walk into it. I've got so much—er . . . I mean *you've* got so much to live for."

"Didn't I tell you?" Suddenly Magnus opens his eyes, sits up, and starts laughing hysterically. "I'm already dead!"

I watch in horror as he grabs the knife and easily slides it out of the wound. Then, incredibly, the gash starts shrinking, before my very eyes. I watch, mesmerized, as an invisible thread seems to sew the skin back together until nothing but a tiny scar remains.

"Oh my God! You're really a . . ." I leap back, horrified. "Oh my God!"

"Sorry," he says, chuckling. "Had to get you back for that bloody finger thing."

I whirl around to find Rayne. She's also cracking up so hard she's practically crying. Like this is the funniest thing she's seen since *Shrek 2*.

"Oh man!" She laughs. "You should have seen your face, Sunny. That was classic!"

I stare at her, then at Magnus. I cannot believe this. I simply cannot believe this. "You . . . I mean . . . I thought . . ." Wow, I've completely lost my ability to talk. I may have to spend the rest of my life as a mute. Walk around with a tablet, writing down everything I used to be able to say, before I was struck dumb by a vampire pulling a knife from his own stomach.

"Sorry," Magnus says, scrambling to his feet. He puts the bloodied knife back into his bag without wiping it. "But you said you wanted proof."

I feel like I'm going to throw up. "So you're really . . ."

". . . a vampire?" he asks, raising an eyebrow. "Yes."

"And that means . . ." My stomach is churning at this point. Like I'm on a storm-tossed ship. Or the Superman ride at Six Flags.

". . . my bite has infected you." He sighs, serious again. "Unfortunately, also yes."

I lean over and throw up.

"Ew." Rayne leaps back to avoid my puke. "Sunny, that's nasty."

"Oh, I'm *so sorry* to have offended you," I say in my most sarcastic tone, wiping my mouth with my sleeve. "I guess I'm not taking the fact that I've been accidentally turned into a freaking vampire as well as you hoped?"

Rayne shrugs. "I totally get it, Sun. Still doesn't mean I enjoy getting splattered by your vomit."

Rolling my eyes, I turn back to Magnus. "So wait a sec," I say. "I'm confused. I always thought that in order to become a vampire, you have to drink the blood of a vampire. All you did was bite me."

"Damn Hollywood and its barbaric misconceptions," Magnus says wearily. He reaches into his mouth and pulls something out. He holds it up to me. It's a porcelain fang, half-filled with red liquid. "Through our postmortem surveys, we've learned that most people find the whole 'drinking blood from their sponsor' part a bit on the disturbing side. Plus," he adds, "while our skin is remarkably good at healing, slicing open one's wrist to enable the apprentice to drink can possibly leave scars. And no one wants a scarred vampire."

He holds out the tooth so I can examine it closer. "So Vamps-R-Us.com created these implants a few years back. Bloody marvelous inventions, really. I just prick my finger, squeeze a few drops of blood into the implant, then inject it into the apprentice." He shrugs. "We could use a syringe to deliver the injection, of course; probably would be easier and more sanitary, actually. But studies have also found that our apprentices enjoy the old-school romanticism of being bitten on the neck."

I can't decide whether I'm more impressed that there are Internet sites that sell blood-injecting gizmos or that these guys ask their victims to fill out feedback forms.

Magnus reaches into his bag and pulls out a small silver case. "Vamps-R-Us.com is the leading manufacturer of vampire supplies. Blood bags, fang sharpeners, body armor, that kind of thing." He opens the case and inserts the fake fang into its velvet lining.

Man, you really *can* buy anything on the Web.

"Okay, gotcha," I say. "But let me ask you this. If I've been turned into a vampire, how come I don't feel like one?"

"How do you know what being a vampire feels like?" Rayne butts in with, unfortunately, a good point.

"Well, I'm not lusting after your blood for one thing," I say slowly. "And, um," I reach under my shirt and pull out my cross necklace. Magnus leaps away. "And the cross doesn't turn me off or burn me or anything." I think for a moment. "And I definitely could go for a slice of cheese and garlic pizza for breakfast as soon as the sun comes out."

Actually the last thing does sound kind of yucky, but I'm not going to admit that to them.

"Could you . . . please . . . put that away?" Magnus asks, gasping for breath.

"So I'm wondering," I say, purposely ignoring him and waving my cross around, watching him dance from side to side to avoid it. "How do we fix this?" I ask.

"F-fix?"

"Yeah. Like stop the transformation. Reverse it. There's gotta be a way to stop it. Right? Maybe suck the blood from the wound like you'd do for a rattlesnake bite?"

I realize Magnus is trying to say something but can't seem to form the words. Oh yeah, the cross. I slip it under my tank. The metal seems a bit warm under my skin, but not uncomfortable. Still, not such a good sign.

"Thank you." Magnus gasps. "Now as I was trying to say, there's no way to reverse it."

"Wrong answer." I reach for my cross.

"Wait!" he cries.

I stop, hand at my throat.

"There . . . might be a way. I'm not sure. I don't know. But Lucifent might."

"Who's this Lucifent guy?"

"My boss. The coven leader. He's a three-thousand-year-old vampire. If anyone knows, he will."

I nod. "Okay. Let's go talk to him."

"We can't. Well, not this second anyway. He's at dinner."

"Yeah, but this is an emergency. Can't we just go hit the restaurant he's at and . . . Oh." I swallow hard. "That kind of dinner?"

Magnus nods.

"Ew."

"Sunny, try to keep an open mind here," Rayne interjects. "Different people have different customs and to ridicule them—"

"So when's he going to be done with his, um, dinner?"

Magnus thinks. "I can call his secretary and see. Maybe he'll have had a cancellation for tomorrow evening, or something. Why don't you meet me in St. Patrick's Cemetery tomorrow at 8 P.M.? I'll be waiting by the big tombstone in the center."

"Tomorrow?" I exclaim. "But that's, like, twenty-four hours from now. I've got school tomorrow."

"So go." Magnus shrugs.

"But won't the sun, like, fry me or something?"

"Look," he says with an exasperated sigh. As if I'm the one inconveniencing him. Jeez. "It takes seven days to complete the transformation into a vampire. So you should be fine. Sun shouldn't bother you too much the first twenty-four hours. Though I would suggest slathering on a little sunscreen, just in case."

Right. Sunscreen and school. This is going to be fun. Not.

5

Boys That Bite: The Blog

You'd think after this drama and unfortunate circumstance, we'd leave Club Fang immediately. But no! When we go back into the club, so Rayne can grab her coat, she insists on doing the Safety Dance before she leaves, saying it's her favorite eighties song in the whole wide world and it'd be cruel and unusual punishment for me to drag her away now. Sure, it's easy for her to shimmy and shake without a care on the dance floor, seeing as she's not the one slowly morphing into a creature of the night. I mean, selfish much?

I'm silent most of the way home, speaking up only to mention that Rayne's selecting the vampire hit "Bela Lugosi's Dead" on her iPod iTrip could be viewed as a tad insensitive, given the circumstances. Of course, she points out that technically Bela was only an actor who played Dracula, not a real vampire. As if that should make me feel better as the chorus chants, "I'm dead, I'm dead, I'm dead, I'm dead."

When I first get home, I want nothing more than to crawl into my bed and sleep. But my heavy feather duvet isn't as comforting as I'd imagined it'd be. I'm wide awake, almost as if I'm hopped up on caffeine. Which is weird, seeing as I didn't even get to drink that Red Bull Rayne was supposed to bring me.

Since I can't sleep, and I have a billion questions buzzing through my brain, I decide my best bet is to go bug Rayne. I push her door open a crack to see if she's sleeping. But she's at her computer, typing furiously, and looking very pissed off. I shake my head. Man, she can be such a freak. I don't know in what Twilight Zone parallel universe we became sisters.

I knock on her door and she calls for me to come in, not looking away from her computer screen. I enter the room and close the door behind me. Luckily, Mom's out at some save-the-planet benefit dinner, so there's no one to overhear us. I'm pretty sure anyone eavesdropping on the convo I plan to have would start speed-dialing the Betty Ford Clinic before you could say *no-I'm-not-on-drugs-I'm-really-an-undead-creature-of-the-night*.

I sit on her bed, marveling how, only hours before, we were joking about what I should wear to Club Fang. If I'd known what repercussions choosing the *Bite Me* tank would have, I'd have definitely swallowed back my good taste and gone with the fetish outfit instead, sweat-inducing vinyl be damned.

After a few more mouse clicks, Rayne turns from her computer and comes to join me on the bed. She's wearing a pair of plaid flannel pajamas and has washed the black makeup from her eyes. With the exception of her tongue piercing, she looks almost normal.

"This sucks," she announces, crossing her legs Indian style.

"You think?" I raise an eyebrow. "'Cause I was totally psyched about the whole thing."

"Not for you, you tool, for me. I've waited freaking years for this night. I've researched, networked, been on waiting lists, the works. And now it's all for nothing."

"What are you talking about?" I know she's speaking English, but nothing she says is making any sense. "Researched and networked for what?"

"To become a vampire, of course."

Of course.

"Why on earth would you want to be a vampire?"

Rayne rolls her eyes, as if to imply I'm the stupidest person on the planet. "Are you kidding me?" she asks incredulously. "Why would I want immortal life? Why would I want riches beyond my wildest imagination? Why would I want ultimate power over mere mortals? You should be asking why anyone on earth *wouldn't* want to be a vampire."

"Yeah, but," I'm grasping at straws here, "don't you want to finish high school? Go to college? Get married, have a life?"

"No."

"No?"

"No way. How boring is that? To conform to society's rigid rules? To be weak and powerless and beaten down and forced to live someone else's idea of a fulfilling life, only to die, sick and alone, and have your grandchildren fight over your meager life's savings? Bleh. No thanks. Give me an all-powerful, immortal existence any day of the week."

Okay, when she puts it that way . . .

"But . . . you have to kill people."

Rayne sighs exasperatedly. "Yeah. So says Hollywood. In real life, Sun, it's a lot less barbaric."

"Oh?"

"Sure. Each vampire is given a stable of donors. People who are willing and able to give a portion of their blood each day so the vampire can survive. Don't worry, they're well paid for their services, and they can sever their contract at any time, by giving thirty days' notice. And of course, they're completely screened and tested for communicable diseases, drugs, that sort of thing, before being assigned." Rayne shakes her head. "No one kills people like in the movies."

"Okay, fine. But what about the sun thing? I can't go out in the daylight, right?"

Rayne examines her powder-white skin. "Yeah. I'd never have to worry about accidentally tanning. Wonderful."

She's thought of everything, hasn't she?

"What about a boyfriend? You'd never get a boyfriend.

You'd never get married. Unless, I guess, you had a night wedding . . ."

"I'd get something better. When someone is selected to become a vampire, he or she is assigned a sponsor," Rayne explains. "The person who has agreed to donate a drop of his or her own blood to aid in your transformation. Afterward, you'll share a blood link with that person forever. He'll be your soul mate. Well, technically your blood mate, as you sort of have to give up that whole soul thing, when you turn." She pauses, staring into the distance, looking a little sad. "Magnus was supposed to be my blood mate. Now he's yours."

Aha! So that's why she's so upset. She thinks I stole her boyfriend. Just goes to show, even in the crazy supernatural world, at the end of the day it all comes down to the green-eyed monster we call jealousy.

"Dude, you can have him," I say, holding my palms out. "I want nothing to do with that jerk."

Rayne turns back to look at me. "You don't understand," she says, her eyes weepy and downcast. "He's turned you. So you're connected. Forever. Whether you like it or not."

"That would be a definite *not*."

"You know, you don't have any clue what a priceless gift you've been given," Rayne says, her voice taking on an irritated edge. "Immortality. The perfect existence. The hottest blood mate to walk the earth. And you're probably more concerned about whether someone's going to ask you to the prom."

"Well, it is this Saturday . . ."

"Man, I can't believe how much this sucks." Rayne angrily swipes her face with her sleeve. Is she crying? Oh man. She *is* crying. She's so totally whacked.

"Look, Rayne," I say, for some inexplicable reason actually feeling the tiniest bit bad for her, "once we get this whole thing reversed, I'm sure you and Magnus can continue your sick and twisted relationship. You can become a vampire and live Gothily ever after."

"I wish." Rayne sniffs. "But no. Even if the process can be reversed, I'll have to start all over. Get back on the waiting list. Find a new sponsor."

"Why?"

"Vampires are allowed to turn only one person in their lifetime. Basically so there's never a blood shortage like the Red Cross always seems to have," she explains. "After they turn the person, they're linked to them forever. Blood mates, until one of them dies."

"Er, how can you die if you have eternal life?"

"Oh, plenty of ways. Burned by sunlight. Caught in a fire. Stabbed with a wooden stake through the heart, you know. All the tragic things that happen in the movies."

Okay, let's take note here: blood-drinking movie clichés, wrong. Methods of killing a vampire, should one be in the position to do so, spot on.

Which brings me to the $64,000 question.

"How do you know all this stuff?"

Rayne shrugs. "Like I said. I've studied. Three months

ago, when I started my training, I actually created a blog to catalog my research." She gestures to her computer. "You should probably check it out. I mean, at the very least it'll outline what you need to know about your transformation. It's kind of bad how unprepared you are. Everyone else that gets turned goes through an extensive three-month certification program."

She's got her Vampire Certificate? Is it suitable for framing?

"I can't believe how organized this whole thing is," I marvel.

"It's a multibillion-dollar operation," Rayne says. "And very high tech." She jumps off the bed and heads over to her computer, clicking on the monitor. "C'mere."

I come behind her and peer at the screen she's brought up. Sure enough, it's some kind of blog, all Gothed out in black and red. I guess the pastel template on Blogspot.com wouldn't really fly for a vampire site.

"Boys That Bite?" I ask, reading the heading.

Rayne giggles. "Yeah, I came up with that name. Funny, huh?"

"I guess." Vampire humor. Hardy har har.

Rayne moves out of her chair and gestures for me to sit down. "Here. Take your time and read. I think you'll learn a lot."

As I plop down in the seat, she walks over to her bookcase and pulls out a heavy hardcover text. "I also have the Vam-

pire 101 textbook you can read. Thank goodness I hadn't returned it to the library yet." She sets the book down on the
desk. "You don't, um, mind picking up the late fees, do you?"

I look down at the massive tome. It's got weird carvings on
the front and has to be like three thousand pages. "Wow. This
vampire thing has a lot of homework involved, doesn't it?"

"Like I said, it's a three-month course. There's a lot to
learn. You're totally going to have to cram at this point."

As if I didn't have enough to worry about, with finals next
week. I flip through the book. Darn, not a lot of pictures either.

"So is this a correspondence course, or do you have to actually attend classes?"

"Classes. After all, you can't learn the proper way to
administer a safe and sterile blood transfusion over the Internet."

"Right." I shake my head, unable to believe I've somehow
gotten mixed up in this freak show. I turn back to the blog
and scroll down to the first entry.

*My name is Rayne McDonald. I'm 16 years old and so
ready for eternal life. As suggested by my instructor, I've
created this blog to chronicle my transformation. Hope
you enjoy reading it!*

Oh, I will. Believe me.

6

Jake Wilder:
Sex God and . . . Prom Date?

After reading some of Rayne's crazy "Boys That Bite" blog and checking out a few links in the vampire Web ring (yes, there really is a vampire Web ring), the bright screen starts giving me a headache. So I say good night to my twin and retreat to the dark safety of my bedroom where I curl up under my duvet and try to go to sleep.

But I can't. I'm too wired with fear and confusion and God knows what else. Plus the spot where Magnus bit me itches like crazy. So I toss and turn and wonder what I'm going to do.

What if the transformation can't be reversed? What if in seven days I, Sunshine McDonald, become a vampire forever? That means no finals. No prom. No sunny trip to the Bahamas with my friends this summer. No college. I'll have to enroll in night school or something. Maybe the vampires have their own university; it does seem like they're pretty organized. I wonder what the SAT requirements are for something like that.

This sucks. Pardon the pun, but it does. I have this whole life ahead of me and now I may not be able to live it, all 'cause of a case of mistaken identity. Damn Rayne and her stupid blog and her stupid idea that becoming undead is the stupid secret to life everlasting. What was she thinking? And why did she have to drag me into it all?

I finally manage to fall asleep, just as the sun peeks over the horizon. In what seems like only five minutes later, my alarm blares me awake with the sounds of the eighties. This morning's DJ chose to wake me with Michael Jackson's "Thriller."

How appropriate.

Groggily, I stumble out of bed and into the shower. It's freezing in the house and the hot water feels good streaming down my body. I try to decide if I feel any different. If I have any urges to suck someone's blood. But no, not yet, at least, thank goodness. Willing donor or not, I'd like to hold off on that part as long as possible, thank you very much. Maybe I could become an anorexic vampire? I wonder if that'd help me shed a few pounds as an added bonus?

I get out of the shower and open the medicine cabinet. A dizzying array of sunscreens stares back at me. From tropical coconut tanning lotions to the no-possible-UV-ray-will-come-within-fifty-yards-of-your-skin-for-three-weeks variety.

Damn me for forgetting to ask Magnus the proper SPF for school.

In the end, I decide to go for the middle-of-the-road 15 stuff. Who knows, maybe I'll get a tan out of the deal. Heh. I'd be the first vampire to look like I'd cruised the Caribbean.

After applying sunscreen, I realize I'll also need to address the bruised purple bite mark on my neck. If anyone sees that they're going to think it's a hickey and I am so not ready to get teased about my neck-munching secret lover, on top of everything else. I guess I could tell everyone I burned my neck with the curling iron, like Mary Markson does when Nick covers her neck with love bites, but no one believes her either.

I rummage through my closet, realizing I own very little clothing designed to cover up my neck. Most likely due to the fact that, before this morning, I had no reason to keep it in hiding. Finally, in the back of my closet, I find an old black turtleneck. I think it belongs to Rayne, actually, but it'll do. Of course everyone's going to think I'm a freak of nature, what with wearing a turtleneck in May. But what can I do? I have become a teenage vampire fashion victim. Ugh.

As long as no one mistakes me for a Goth . . .

School is okay, though I'm so freaking tired, it's hard to pay attention. And I seem to have become a magnet for teacher questions. I go rest my eyes for one teensy second and suddenly

I'm harassed to start calculating pi or something. (Which I can't even do on a full night of sleep when I'm not transforming into a vampire.)

I eat lunch with a few girls from field hockey, picking listlessly at my salad as I halfheartedly listen to them recount last week's game. My other teammates are so wrapped up in their tales of opposing goalkeeper Jennifer Jack spraining her ankle in the first five minutes of the game that they don't notice I'm barely listening. Which is fine by me. The last thing I need to do is draw attention to myself in my current state.

Luckily, my best friend Audrey is away this week at Disney World with her parents. The girl is so scarily perceptive that she'd notice something was wrong immediately. At the same time, she'd never believe the whole vampire thing and would think I had really lost it. So while I'd love to have some moral support (Rayne so doesn't count!) it's probably better off I don't freak out my friends.

I consider skipping drama practice after school, but Magnus has informed me he won't be up and about till almost eight P.M., so I figure I might as well go and kill time before my big meeting with the head vamp. Besides, this way I can have some quality Jake Wilder spyage time. Bound to make anyone feel better.

Ah, Jake Wilder. How do I even explain the greatness that is Jake Wilder? It's like he doesn't belong in a normal, everyday high school. Like, he should have been born centuries earlier, in Roman times or something—driving a flaming chariot with six white horses foaming at the mouth. He looks like a Greek god, with his six-foot-one stance, slender but muscular body, and high cheekbones. Well, a Greek god or Chad Michael Murray, take your pick. He has short blond hair and the deepest, darkest brown eyes known to mankind. I once overheard some girls calling him Bedroom Eyes.

I'd love to see those bedroom eyes actually in a bedroom. Preferably my bedroom. In fact, if I could have me some of that, I'd so retire my Sunny the Innocent status, quicker than you can say "off like a prom dress."

Problem is, he has no idea I even exist. None whatsoever. I blame Heather Miller.

You see, Jake Wilder is the leading man, the sexy Conrad Birdie, in our class production of *Bye Bye Birdie* this year. And Heather is, of course, playing Kim. No surprise there. No matter what play we do, Heather nabs the starring role. *Little Shop of Horrors*? She's Audrey. *Oklahoma*? She's Laurey. In second grade we performed *The Tortoise and the Hare* and Jake got the tortoise and she was the hare. She's Drama Queen with a capital DQ. Beautiful. Blond. Busty. Even brainy, if you can believe that. You'd at least hope she'd be an airhead, but no. No, she's also president of the Honor Society, which is so not fair to the rest of us mere mortals.

This year, I didn't even get awarded a small part in the play. Not even some one-line Conrad Birdie groupie role. Nada. Instead, I'm Heather Miller's understudy. Meaning I have to do all the work, memorize all the lines, and only if Miss Perfect-Attendance-Award is sick do I get to take center stage.

Which is actually not as terrible as it sounds, seeing as I have rather a bad case of stage fright and if I were to be suddenly thrust into the starring role, I'm not positive I could handle it.

For me, drama is all about permission to stare at Jake Wilder for hours on end without anyone thinking me Stalker Girl.

So with that in mind, I slip into the second-to-last row of the school auditorium and pull out my sketchpad. Back here, no one can see what I'm drawing. I get so much crap for being an artist you wouldn't believe it. No respect at all.

"Sunshine McDonald? Is that you?"

I look up from my drawing, a rather brilliant sketch of Jake Wilder if I do say so myself. The drama teacher, Mr. Teifert, is down by the stage and motioning for me to join him.

O-kay. That's weird. I wasn't convinced he even knew my name, never mind that he'd ever need to get my attention. I slip my sketchbook back into my book bag and trudge to the front of the auditorium, a little wary.

"Sunshine. Thank goodness you're here," Mr. Teifert says, rubbing a hand through his wild black curly hair. He's short and squat and looks like that guy from *Animal House*. "Heather's sick. We need you to stand in for her at practice today."

I stare at him, at first not quite comprehending. The queen

has lost her attendance throne? And they need me to step in? Wow. I wasn't expecting that to happen. Especially not today, when I have so much else on my mind.

"O-kay," I say, swallowing down the bubble of stage fright that immediately forms in my stomach and starts traveling up my esophagus. "What scene are we working on?"

"The one where Birdie kisses Kim," says a deep, luscious man-voice behind me.

I whirl around and almost pass out when I realize the delectable Jake Wilder is standing there, in the flesh, not two feet away, actually speaking to me. And using the word *kiss* in a sentence. A sentence addressed to me.

"Kisses Kim?" I manage to speak in my Minnie Mouse voice. *Nice, Sunny.* So very attractive and appealing.

"Don't look so horrified," Mr. Teifert says with a laugh.

I look horrified because I just sounded like a moron, not because of the proposition of kissing Jake Wilder. That's not horror. That's romance. A fantasy dream come true. But I can't exactly explain that, now can I?

"I'm fine. Let's do it," I say, forcing my voice to go back to normal. I hop up onto the stage, my legs literally trembling in a way I hope isn't noticeable. Jake pops up a moment later and now stands facing me.

"Okay, now the scene is, Conrad and Kim are in rehearsals for *The Ed Sullivan Show.* Sunny, you recite your Conrad Birdie fan club speech, then Jake, you're bored with this and want to go party, so you interrupt, yada yada yada, then kiss her. Ronald," Mr. Teifert looks over at the tall skinny boy who's playing Kim's boyfriend, Hugo. "You're on the balcony, glaring at Birdie, really jealous like. After the kiss, Sunny, you collapse in a faint."

Fainting after Jake Wilder's kiss? Shouldn't be too tough to make that look realistic!

Mr. Teifert claps his hands. "Got it? Then places, everyone."

And so it goes. I pledge my devotion to Conrad Birdie a.k.a. Jake Wilder. And he interrupts, then scoops me in his arms and kisses me, hard on the mouth.

Time seems to stop.

I let out an unwilling gasp as he presses his firm lips against mine. I never, ever thought I'd get a chance to feel what it'd be like for Jake Wilder to kiss me. And it feels better than I could have imagined in my wildest of dreams.

He pauses for a moment, as if surprised about something, then takes advantage of my parted mouth and enters it with his tongue. Aghh! What an incredible feeling. I feel like I'm going to explode, it feels so good. Jake Wilder is kissing me. French-kissing me. Is he even supposed to be French-kissing me for the play? I thought . . . Oh, who cares if he's supposed to or not. He is, that's all that matters.

"Hey, guys, okay, already. You're supposed to faint, Sunny." Mr. Teifert's voice sounds a million miles away.

Jake pulls away, reluctantly, it seems. Our faces are inches apart still—I can feel his hot, minty breath in my face. Then he gives me a small grin and whispers, "I think we need more practice," so softly only I can hear. "Don't you?"

Then I faint. Or at least I fake fainting, though actually I feel like I could almost lose consciousness for real after what just happened. Jake Wilder, kissing me. Sure, it was just for the play, but somehow it felt like more than that. It felt like he enjoyed it.

I know I did.

Thank you, Heather, for being absent. Thank you, thank you, thank you. This makes every boring rehearsal, every wasted understudy hour, worth it.

And the best thing is, we have to do it all over again. Several times. Practice makes perfect, you know.

After the rehearsal is over, I climb down off the stage and head to the back, where I've left my book bag. My legs feel like Jell-O.

"Hey, Sunny!"

I turn around, bag in my hands at the voice. I force my mouth not to drop open in shock as I realize who's come up behind me.

"Hey Jake," I say shyly, dropping my gaze. Gah, he's so cute. I can barely stand it. How can one guy be so gifted in the looks department? I mean, even Zac Efron's got nothing on Jake Wilder.

Jake runs a hand through his hair, for some reason appearing a little nervous. Weird. I should be the one who's shaking like a leaf here, not him.

"You were, um, great up there," he says, shuffling from foot to foot.

I beam at the compliment. I know it's uncool to be so psyched about it, but I can't help it. Jake Wilder has just said I was great. I, Sunshine McDonald, was great in the eyes of Jake Wilder.

"Thanks," I say in my most casual of tones. "You were great, too. I can see why you always get the lead."

He shrugs. "Yeah, I guess," he says, clearing his throat. I look at him curiously. He's not acting like his usual overconfident popular self at all. What's up with that? "But you, you were a goddess."

A goddess? What is that supposed to mean? I know I nailed the dance number, but I didn't think I was especially goddesslike doing it. I narrow my eyes, not quite sure if he's making fun of me. Maybe this is one of those cruel jokes that the popular kids always seem to play in the movies. Bet the football star he can't get Loser Nerd Girl to fall in love with him. Well, I'm sooo not falling for that.

"Uh-huh. Goddess. Right." I snort. "Yeah, I've always kind of thought of myself as a teenage Artemis, now that you mention it." I grab my coat. After all that's taken place in the last twenty-four hours, I am so not in the mood to be made fun of by the guy I'm stalking. "In fact, I've got some goddess-type duties to take care of now, so I'll, um, catch you around." I start to maneuver around him.

He steps in front of me. "Wait," he says.

I wait. My heart is pounding in my chest now. This is too weird.

"Um, I wanted to uh, ask you if . . ." He clears his throat again. Does he have a cold or something? "If you have a date for the prom, and if you don't do you want to go with me?" he blurts out, in one big run-on sentence.

I stare at him, doing everything in my power not to gape with an open mouth. Did he just say what I thought he said? Did he just . . . no, I must have heard wrong.

"Wh-what?" I ask, squeaky Minnie Mouse voice back with a vengeance.

He blushes a deep red. Jake Wilder. Blushing. Have we entered a parallel universe here? I remind myself this could all be some cruel prank. That I may get to the prom and the Populars will pull a Carrie and pour pig's blood on me when I'm voted prom queen. And I won't even have the telekinetic power to burn down the school in vengeance.

But that's stupid. I may not be head cheerleader, but I'm certainly not Loser Nerd Girl either. I have tons of friends and play on the varsity field hockey team. So I highly doubt I'd be top of the list for the Populars to pick on.

Besides, Jake seems deadly serious.

"I just thought, if you weren't going with anyone, that you might, uh, want to go with, um, me," he continues, stammering. "I mean, if you wanted to. I understand if you don't. Obviously you've probably got like three million guys asking you."

I nearly fall backward into a dead faint for real this time. As it is, I'm not quite sure my heart is still beating.

Jake Wilder has just asked me to the prom. Jake Wilder!

"Uh, yeah. Sure. That's cool," I say with a shrug, awarding myself major brownie points for not jumping up and down and doing cartwheels down the auditorium aisle. "Why not?"

He breaks out into his amazing smile, looking oh-so-relieved. "Great," he says. "Really great. Thank you. I'll um, see you around then."

"Uh, sure. Okay," I say at a loss for more intellectual conversation. *Real suave, Sunny.*

He smiles at me again—that infamous brilliant flash of Jake Wilder pearly whites—then turns and bolts out of the auditorium. I stare after him, confused as anything.

Jake Wilder has just asked me to the prom. And I said yes. Before today I would have bet anything that he didn't even know my name. Now I'm suddenly his prom date?

"Hey, Sunny, how you feeling?"

I turn around. Rayne's entered the auditorium.

"Rayne!" I cry. "You'll never guess! Jake Wilder asked me to the prom. Isn't that so amazing? I mean, Jake Wilder! Can you believe it? I'm freaking out here!"

Rayne smiles her favorite patronizing smile. "Ah, the Vampire Scent is already kicking in, huh?"

I screw up my face. "Vampire Scent?" What the hell is she talking about? And what does that have to do with Jake asking me to the prom?

"Yeah, you know. Like pheromones. Vampires give off a scent that drives mere mortals crazy with desire. They can't resist it. It's actually very useful when talking your way out of speeding tickets or scoring an aisle seat on an airplane. Though the old lady the next seat over talking to you about her grandchildren the whole flight can be an unfortunate side effect."

My heart sinks. To my toes.

So evidently Jake Wilder hasn't lusted after me for years and only now gotten up the courage to approach me.

"Damn." I kick the auditorium seat in frustration. "And here I thought he had some secret crush on me or something." I sigh. I knew it was too good to be true.

"Jeez, Sunny, don't act so disappointed. I mean, didn't you read about all this in my blog last night?"

Uh-oh.

"I, uh, didn't finish reading the whole thing. I mean, it was pretty long."

Rayne stares at me. "The pheromone thing is like the third entry down."

"Yeah, but," I can feel my face heating up. "There were these links and . . ."

"Links?"

"Yeah, to really good stories about Spike and Angel . . ."

"So let me get this straight," Rayne says, crossing her arms over her chest, looking very unhappy. "Instead of catching up on the vital information you need to know about your impending vampire transformation, you instead chose to read *Buffy the Vampire Slayer* fanfic?"

Okay, when she puts it that way, it does seem like a bad decision on my part. But some of those stories were way juicy and . . .

"You know, you shouldn't have links on your Web site if you don't want people to click on them," I say in my defense.

Rayne sighs. Deeply. "You know, I really hope that Lucifent has a way to turn you back into a human. 'Cause you're going to totally suck as a vampire."

I start laughing. I can't help it. I'm going to *suck* as a vampire? Ha!

"What?" Rayne demands. Then she realizes her unintentional pun. "Oh." She tries to frown, but I can see the corners of her mouth turn up. "This is serious, Sunny."

"I know!" I cry, still howling with laughter. The whole situation's suddenly struck me as so absurd that I can't help it. "I'm going to be a SUCKY vampire!"

Rayne bursts into laughter. "Talk about a Freudian slip! I can't believe I said that."

"Yeah, well being a vampire really BITES," I add, bringing on a whole new wave of laughter. We're practically crying and rolling in the aisle, we're cracking up so bad.

"Who's a vampire?"

A deep voice cuts through our laughing and sobers us up immediately. We both whirl around to see Mr. Teifert, the drama teacher, peering at us curiously behind his black-rimmed glasses. I guess we were laughing so hard we didn't even hear him approach.

Rayne smiles wickedly. "Sunny's a vampire," she says. "Well, she's on her way to being one." Then she starts laughing again. I kick her in the ankle to make her shut up. While I'm about one hundred percent positive Mr. Teifert will take her claim with a grain of dramatic salt, I've still got to work with the guy on the school play. I don't want him to think I'm some stupid ditz. Then he'll never give me a good part and I'll be in understudy world forever.

Mr. Teifert raises a bushy eyebrow. "Is this true, Sunny?" he asks in a voice that seems far too serious for the discussion. What's his deal? "Are you a vampire?"

Thank goodness I wore a turtleneck to school so he can't see the bruised, hickeylike bite on my neck. Then he'd really be speed-dialing the guidance counselor.

"No, Mr. Teifert," I say, forcing myself to keep a straight face. "I am not a vampire. We were just messing around."

His serious expression relaxes and he smiles. "Good to know. Especially since we need you for this play. I've just learned Heather has come down with mono and won't be back. So from this point on, you'll be playing the part of Kim."

I restrain myself from giving a loud "Woot!" right then and there and try to look like I'm concerned for poor little Heather Miller. But to hell with her! I'm now the star of the school play. How cool is that? You know, besides the whole vampire thing being a downer, the rest of my life sure seems to be turning around in a big way, go figure.

"Thanks, Mr. Teifert. I won't let you down," I tell him enthusiastically.

"I know you won't," he says with a wink. "Just promise you won't go turning into a vampire on me. We've got a lot of rehearsals and most of them are during the day."

"I, uh, won't." I say, laughing my nervous donkey bray. As if what he's saying is the silliest thing in the entire universe.

He nods and smiles and waves good-bye as he exits the auditorium. Rayne and I exchange looks and then grab our book bags and hustle out.

"That was kinda weird," I say, as we head out into the parking lot toward our car.

"That was more than weird," Rayne agrees. She rummages around in her purse for the car keys. "You need to be careful around him."

"Oh, I'm sure he just overheard us and thought it'd be funny to join in on the joke."

Rayne pulls out the keys by her spider key chain. "I don't know, Sunny. I get creepy vibes off him." She unlocks the door and hops in the car.

I join her and take a seat in the passenger side. "What are you, a vibe reader now?" I ask skeptically. "He's a teacher. He thought he was being funny. You're paranoid."

Rayne shrugs as she puts the key in the ignition. "Okay,

Sun, fine. I'm only trying to look out for you. There's a lot of vampire prejudice out there, you know." She pauses. "Actually you *don't* know," she adds, "since you'd rather read the sexploits of Spike and Buffy than research the subject."

"I actually preferred the stories about Angel." I giggle.

Rayne shakes her head. "See what I mean?" she says, sounding more than a little frustrated. "You refuse to take anything I say seriously. I don't know why I'm bothering to help you. I should just leave you to flounder and figure it all out yourself."

She looks seriously mad, so I decide to throw her a bone. After all, I need a ride to the cemetery to meet Magnus.

"I'm sorry, Rayne. I know you're trying to help me," I say in the most sincere voice I can muster. "It's just sometimes I use humor to defuse a tense, stressful situation." Wow, I sound like I should be on *Dr. Phil.* "I do appreciate you helping me, though. More than you know."

"Well, you are my little sister," Rayne hedges.

"Yes, by seven whole minutes. Making you way more older, wiser, and worldly than I could ever hope to be."

Rayne shoots me a look.

I laugh. "Sorry."

"Okay, let's get to the cemetery," she says. "And see if we can't get this vampire thing reversed."

"Sounds like a plan."

Rayne pulls out of the parking lot and takes a left. We're silent for a moment. Then . . .

"Do you think if I change back into a human, Jake will revoke his invitation to the prom?"

"Arghh!"

"Sorry." I fold my hands in my lap and make like a good, silent, serious vampire-chick-to-be.

I do wonder, though.

7

The Coven— a.k.a. Kick-Ass Underground Mansion

We pull into St. Patrick's Cemetery, driving between two dead-Catholic-guy statues flanking the entryway and down a narrow road lined by gravestones.

"You know, meeting with a vampire in a cemetery seems such a cliché," I note as I stare out the window, trying not to let the gravestones creep me out too much.

Rayne shrugs. "You'd know why if you read my blog, but hey, I'm sure that fanfic was real enthralling."

"Will you cut the 'if you read my blog' crap?" I beg, rolling my eyes at her. "I mean, honestly. I will read the thing. From start to finish, I promise you. But I couldn't exactly have read it between drama class and our trip to the cemetery, now could I?"

"Fine, fine." Rayne turns the steering wheel so the car pulls to the side of the road. She kills the engine. "We're here anyway."

I look around. We're surrounded by gravestones, far as the eye can see, which is, I might add, a tad disconcerting, given the circumstances.

"We're here? Where's Magnus?"

Bang! Bang!

A sudden knock on the window I'm peering out of makes me practically jump out of my skin. I see a head duck down and peek in.

Speak of the devil.

I roll down the window. "Jeez, Magnus," I grumble. "You practically gave me a heart attack. Sneak up much?"

He grins, not looking at all broken up about scaring me half to death. "We vampires are quite good at coming and going without being noticed."

Okay, add super stealth to the list of vampire powers. Probably used to help them hunt humans before they got that whole donor blood bank thing worked out. You know, they should become assassins for the government or something. Sneak into Afghanistan and drain Bin Laden dry.

Hmm. Maybe they already have and that's why no one can find the guy . . .

"Uh, are you ready to go, or would you prefer to sit in the car making mad faces a bit longer?" Magnus asks sweetly.

"Hold your fangs, will you?" I shoot him a dirty look as

I push the car door open, feeling a slight rush of satisfaction when it hits him in the shin. (Even though it probably just slightly tickles, him being a vampire and all.)

I step out of the car and turn back to Rayne. "You coming?"

She frowns. "I'm not invited."

What? She's planning on leaving me alone with this irritating bloodsucker? Annoying twin sister or not, there's no freaking way I'm down with that.

"Yes, you are," I say. "You're totally invited. I'm inviting you. I'll have an invitation printed up, in fact, if that helps. Or how about an Evite?"

"No." That negative coming from the irritating bloodsucker in question, not my poor uninvited twin.

"No? What do you mean, no?" I say, turning to him, hands on my hips.

"Sunny, I can't come. Only vampires get to enter the sacred coven."

"Can't you make an exception? A special dispensation?" I put on my best pleading face. The one that always gets me the car on school nights when my mom thinks I should be studying. "Please? She's my twin sister. And after all, she knows way more about being a vampire than I do. She even has a blog about the whole thing." I turn back to Rayne, giving her a sneaky smile. "Which I totally plan on reading the second I get home."

"No." Magnus huffs loudly. As if I'm a pain in the neck to

him and not the other way around. "She can't come. There are rules. Rules that have been in existence for thousands of years."

"Rules, schmules," I mutter halfheartedly. I know I've lost. I glance over to Rayne, who also looks slightly hurt and disappointed. I'm sure she was hoping to get a firsthand glimpse of this coven place. Like seeing Disney World or something to her vampire-obsessed eyes.

"Sorry, Rayne," I say, leaning into the car. "Thanks for the ride, though."

"Do you want me to wait for you?"

"Sur—"

"No." From Magnus, of course. He really likes that word. I can tell. He must have been such fun as a toddler. "I do not know how long we will be. I will take Sunshine home when we are done."

I raise an eyebrow. "Okay, fine. As long as it doesn't involve turning into a bat and flying home or something." Actually that might kinda rock, but I'm not admitting that to him.

"Uh, no. It'd be in a Jaguar XKR convertible if milady dost approve of that," he corrects, in a mocking voice.

Oh. "Uh, yeah. I guess that'd be okay," I say, though inside I'm doing the Snoopy dance. A ride in a Jaguar convertible? How cool is that? Way cooler than bat flying, IMO. And certainly better than our beat-up Volkswagen bug.

Cheered, I say good-bye to my disappointed twin and follow Magnus into the darkness. At first I'm a bit creeped out as we wander through the moonlit graveyard, but then I realize the place's only real-life monster is already on my team, so I'm probably pretty safe.

We come to a huge, ornate tomb in the center of the cemetery. I mean, this thing is big enough to walk in and has a door and everything. It totally dwarfs the rest of the cemetery and looks really out of place looming in the center of it.

I watch as Magnus stops at the tomb and produces a golden key from around his neck. I'd been so annoyed before that I hadn't totally checked him out. Not that I should bother, but loser or not, he is *such* good eye candy. Tonight he's got this total Euro look going on; he's wearing a leather jacket over a black Armani turtleneck that hugs his perfectly sculptured chest, and distressed, low-rise Diesel jeans that hug, well, you know, everything else. His shiny chestnut-colored, Orlando Bloom hair is pulled back with a black leather tie, definitely giving him the rebellious pirate look. In short, he looks De-lish with a capital D.

It really is too bad he's the bane of my existence and all.

Magnus inserts the key into the lock and the tomb's heavy marble door creeks open on rusty hinges. We step inside and the musty smell immediately takes over my senses. I start to sneeze.

When I do, my vampire guide doesn't say *bless you*, and at first I contemplate berating him for his lack of manners. Then I realize it's probably too religious for a vampire to say and decide to cut him some slack this time. (Though he could have at least ventured a *Gesundheit,* IMO.)

The door closes behind us and for a moment we're blanketed by darkness. O-kay. Kind of freaky. I'm now standing in an actual tomb, in pitch darkness, with only a vampire to keep me company. Last week if you'd sworn on a stack of Bibles that I'd be okay with all of this, I wouldn't have believed you.

Magnus feels around for my hand and then, finding it, latches on and leads me into the darkness. And yes, regrettably, I must admit that his touch sends an unwilling chill up my spine.

Thanks a lot, body. Betray your owner much?

"Watch the stairs," he says as we step down. Are we going underground? Curiouser and curiouser, as Alice in Wonderland would say.

We descend. Step after step after step. How deep are we going? It feels like I'm walking down the Empire State Building or something. They should install elevators in this place. What if they turned a handicapped person into a vampire? Talk about your discrimination lawsuit waiting to happen.

"You all right?" Magnus asks softly, his husky British accent cutting through the darkness.

"Yeah," I whisper back. "I'm good."

Okay, fine. I admit it. The situation is kind of intimate and I'm sort of turned on. I mean, no matter how annoying

Magnus is, he's also indescribably hot. And having an inde-scribably hot guy holding my hand and leading me blindly through the darkness is sort of sexy in a very weird way.

Gah! I can't believe I just admitted that! When I'm done with this vampire nonsense, I've so got to get my head exam-ined. After all, I do not think of Magnus in that way. I think of Jake Wilder, my prom date, in that way. Jake Wilder only. Not Magnus. Definitely not Magnus.

After half an eternity, we finally reach the end of the never-ending stairs and I can hear Magnus pressing some computerized buttons. Like a key code or something. This vampire place has major security.

A door slides silently open and we step over the threshold. Into complete luxury.

I gasp as my eyes become accustomed to the dim light and I see what we've walked into. It's like a mansion. An un-derground mansion. With cathedral ceilings, floors made of marble, and the most elegant furnishings I've ever seen. I can see why they need Fort Knox–like security down here. It's a tomb raider's dream come true. Lara Croft would have a field day.

"Holy hot spot, Batman," I whisper.

Magnus grins. "Impressive, no? We vampires like our lit-tle creature comforts."

I scan the room, taking in the velvet antique couches and gold-accented lamps. The Da Vinci paintings and crystal chandeliers. This place is like Buckingham Palace. If not more luxurious.

"Guess you guys aren't putting any strain on the welfare system, at least."

"When you live thousands of years, your investments tend to mature and pay off nicely."

"Evidently." Rayne sure wasn't kidding when she said riches greater than your wildest imagination. Maybe this being a vampire thing isn't as bad as I thought. First, you have hot guys throwing themselves at you, then you have enough cash to buy every shoe Marc Jacobs ever made.

Pretty sweet. Too bad there's also the whole blood-drinking and no-going-out-in-the-sun side effects. Otherwise, I'd definitely have to reconsider this whole thing.

"Come on," Magnus says, interrupting my musings. "Lucifent is expecting us."

8

Lucifent—King of Vamps and Major Cutie Pie

I follow Magnus across the empty hall, wondering where the other vampires are hiding. Or feeding. *Gulp.* The thought makes me walk faster to catch up to his long strides.

We head down a long corridor, flanked by dim lamps. Nothing in the place is particularly bright, I notice. Probably hard on the vamps' eyes.

At the end of the hall, we enter a lobby where a thin, blond woman sits behind a desk, filing her nails and looking bored. She looks like someone I know, but I can't seem to place her.

"Hi, Marcia," Magnus says, addressing her politely.

That's it! She looks like Marcia Brady from the *The Brady Bunch.* Heh.

Marcia looks up, her eyes widening in delight as they fall on Magnus. "Oh, Magnus!" she cries, her voice high and flirty and American. "It's sooo great to see you! It's been way too long, my darling."

Hmm. Guess this guy's not only hot stuff to us mortals. He's got vamp groupies as well. Go figure. I squash a brief pang of jealousy. Which is ridiculous. After all, blood mate or not, I so don't want to have anything to do with Magnus after we get this vampire thing sorted out. So if Marcia wants him, he's all hers, far as I'm concerned.

I tune back in to the conversation.

"It's lovely to see you as well, Marcia darling," Magnus says in his deep, baritone voice. "How have you been?"

The vampire secretary blushes furiously. Man, she's got it bad! Marcia, Marcia, Marcia! "Very well, thank you," she says and then giggles.

This is all making me feel like I want to hurl.

"Uh, hello?" I interject, to stave off the nauseated feeling. "I don't have all night."

Marcia shoots me an evil glare. "Who is this?" she asks, haughtily. "Another recruit? We *are* going bottom-of-the-barrel these days, aren't we?"

"Excuse me?" I say, raising an eyebrow. "Would you mind repeating that?" Vampire or no, I'm so not taking this bitch's attitude.

"Ladies, please," Magnus says, looking pained. "Marcia, we're here to speak with Lucifent. Is he ready to see us?"

Marcia shoots me one last glare, then sulkily presses an intercom button on her phone. "Your eight o'clock is here," she mutters.

"Send them in."

She nods her head toward the ornate mahogany door behind her. "He's all yours."

I follow Magnus as he opens the door and heads into the rear office, stopping only for a moment to stick my tongue out at Marcia. Childish, I know, but oh so satisfying.

The bee-yotch flips me the bird.

Lucifent's office turns out to be as deluxe as the rest of the underground coven. The only thing missing is windows. I'd hate the no-windows thing, were I to become a permanent vamp. Though the Picassos on the wall might make up for their absence somewhat. The floors are made of gleaming hardwood and a giant mahogany desk lies in the center of the room.

Behind the desk sits Haley Joel Osment, the little kid from that creepy *Sixth Sense* movie.

Okay, maybe it's not Haley Joel himself. But this kid looks a lot like him—has the whole blond hair, wide eyes thing going on. Definitely a cutie pie. Must be Lucifent's kid or something. I mean, who knows, maybe it's Take Your Son to Work Day on the vampire calendar.

"Hey you," I say, crouching down to smile at him. I love children. So sweet and innocent and full of life before age jades them into sullen, sarcastic brats who would sell their own mothers for a nickel bag of pot. "You're so cute. I bet your daddy is really proud of you. How old are you now?"

"Oh, about three thousand, give or take a hundred," the kid snarls, his happy baby face morphing into a very pissed-off look. "Magnus," he rages. "What is the meaning of this?"

Have you ever seen that cartoon *Family Guy* with that baby, Stewie, who talks like he's an adult and constantly tries to take over the world? That's sort of what this kid is reminding me of all of a sudden.

I glance over at Magnus, who looks angry and frightened and nervous all at the same time.

"I am very sorry, my lord," he says, bowing low to the kid. "She doesn't know."

O-kay then. I'm totally lost here. I really should have read that stupid blog.

Magnus rises from his reverential bow and turns to face me. "Sunny," he hisses in a tight voice. "This is Lord Lucifent, leader of the Blood Coven. High priest of the eastern vampire conglomerate of the United States of America."

I raise an eyebrow and glance over at the kid sitting behind the enormous desk. "Haley Joel Osment here is your fearless leader?" I start to laugh. I can't help it. It's just so funny to think of this little Dennis the Menace look-alike as the leader of the vampires. Soon I'm laughing so hard tears are falling down my cheeks. This is who everyone is scared of? The almighty Lucifent? I can barely resist the urge to go over and pinch the little rascal's cheeks.

"Can you please shut her up?" Lucifent demands in an adorable squeaky little-boy voice. Heh. He looks positively livid. So does Magnus for that matter.

"Sunny, listen to me," Magnus says in a snarly voice. A voice way more intimidating than little Lucifent's. "Unless you are happy with the idea of remaining a vampire for the rest of your life, I suggest you stop laughing this instant."

Oh. Okay, if you put it that way . . . I swallow back my giggles and adopt my most serious expression. "Sorry," I mutter.

"Now bow to Lucifent," Magnus hisses from the corner of his mouth. "And pay your respects to our lord."

Oh, jeez Louise! But I guess, whatever it takes, right? I drop a little curtsy, feeling somewhat ridiculous.

"Who is this ignorant woman, Magnus, and why have you brought her to me?" demands Lucifent. "I am appalled by this show of disrespect."

Magnus shuffles from foot to foot. "Well, you see, sir, there's been, a, um . . ."

"Case of mistaken identity," I state, figuring he needs some help spitting it out.

Magnus shoots me a tortured glare, not looking at all grateful for my assistance in explaining the situation. Wow, he seems really nervous. And he's usually so confident. Arrogant even. This Lucifent guy, cute kid or no, must be real powerful in vamp circles. He's like a mafia Godfather or something.

"What do you mean, case of mistaken identity?" Luficent questions in a tight voice.

"Well, th-this is Sunshine McDonald," Magnus says, gesturing to me. "And she has a, um, identical twin sister named Rayne."

"And I care about their family tree, why?"

Magnus swallows hard. "Her twin went through all the training. She was assigned to me as my blood mate."

"And?" Lucifent's face has gone quite pink. I think he's finally getting the gist of what Magnus is saying. For king of the vampires, he comes off a bit slow, if you ask me.

"And I bit the wrong twin." Magnus admits, dropping his eyes to the floor, his face blazing red with embarrassment.

"You what?" Lucifent cries, even angrier now than he was at my laughing. Magnus flinches as if he's been struck. "You bit the wrong person? Someone who didn't sign a release? Who didn't get tested first? Who didn't go through the training?" He slams a tiny fist against the desk and I stifle another giggle. I can't help it, he's just so darn cute. "How could you, Magnus? You worthless bag of bones! You're useless! Why, I should have left you to rot in that Moorish prison. I gave you eternal life. Riches beyond belief. Power beyond a mortal's imagination. And this is how you repay me?"

Magnus looks like he wants to crawl under the desk and die. I almost feel bad for him. I mean, hey, I don't like that he screwed this up as much as the next guy, probably more even, seeing as it directly affects me and my life. But still, we all make mistakes. No need for this verbal bashing. I wonder if vampires have unions. Magnus could so report this guy.

"Look, dude, it's really not Magnus's fault," I butt in, attempting to defuse some of Lucifent's rage. He definitely has major anger management issues he needs to deal with. "I mean, Rayne and I look exactly identical. Even our mom can't tell us apart."

"Shut up, human," Lucifent snarls. Evidently he didn't rise to king of the vampires on the basis of his charm alone.

"I am sorry, my lord," Magnus says, bowing low. "I know I made a terrible mistake. And I'm willing to pay the price."

"That's good of you. Because you *will* pay, for certain," Lucifent agrees with a self-satisfied smirk. As if he's enjoying Magnus's distress. Loser. "You will pay well."

"You know, assigning blame's all fine and good," I interrupt. "But we need to move on here and get more solution oriented. In six days, I'm told I'll be changing into a vampire, unless this whole thing is reversed. So I'm here to find out how the whole reversal thing works. Tell me that, and I'll be on my merry way."

"Anything for that to happen," mutters Lucifent. "Very well, then. I will tell you what you must do."

9

Bertha the Vampire Slayer

"So there *is* a way?" I ask, trying not to get too excited. "The transformation can be reversed?"

Lucifent nods. "Indeed," he says. "It's simple, really. All you have to do is—"

Suddenly, milliseconds before he can spit out the knowledge that will save me from eternal damnation, warning sirens start going off. They sound like something you'd hear on a *Star Trek* episode, moments before the *Enterprise* self-destructs. Or after Homer Simpson does something stupid yet again at the Springfield nuclear power plant.

"The perimeter has been breached," a robotic female voice announces, her tone oddly calm and computerized, given her message. "The Slayer has entered the building."

Lucifent utters a curse that no Haley Joel look-alike should ever utter, as it's quite disconcerting to anyone in the vicinity. Then he leaps from his desk, his eyes wide with fright.

"We've got to get to the safe room!" he cries, running toward the door.

"Wait," I call, struggling to be heard over the chaos. "What about turning me back to a human?"

"Later!" Magnus says, sounding just as panicked as he grabs my arm and hustles me toward the door. "We've got to hide from Bertha."

"Bertha?"

"Yes, Bertha," he repeats impatiently, dragging me out of the office. "Bertha the Vampire Slayer."

Hmm. Doesn't have the same ring to it as her TV counterpart. But okay, whatever.

I follow Magnus down the ornate hallway, quickly catching up to and then passing Lucifent, whose little legs can't take big strides like ours.

"Hurry, Master," Magnus begs.

"The Slayer has entered the sanctuary," the female computer announces, helpfully.

"Phew." Magnus stops running, allowing Lucifent to catch up. "She's on the other side of the compound. It'll take her at least ten minutes to get over here."

Lucifent nods. "We should still get to the—"

"The Slayer has entered the east hallway."

Hmm. Either the Slayer is superfast or there's been some

kind of glitch in the Matrix. 'Cause suddenly, a woman drops down from a grate in the ceiling, effectively blocking our path.

She's dressed in black leather, but don't get the mistaken impression that she's at all attractive and sexy in it. Let's just say Bertha the Vampire Slayer has evidently been hitting the drive-through a few too many times on her dinner break. And leather sure isn't very forgiving when it comes to super sizing your French fries. Especially tight, low-rise leather pants that allow her stomach fat to ooze out her front. Add a greasy zit-face and the stringy blond hair and you'll get a good mental picture of what this "Slayer" looks like.

I think I prefer Sarah Michelle Gellar.

"Lucifent," she snarls, raising her wooden stake. Wow, she's got braces too. I can't believe the mortal enemy of all vampires goes to an orthodontist. "Prepare to die."

Then, without further ado and quicker than my eyes can follow, Bertha back-handsprings down the hallway, flabby flesh flopping around like a fish out of water. For someone so anorexically challenged, the girl can really move!

Then she stakes Lucifent in the heart.

There's no dramatic fight scene. No exchange of clever banter. Just stakeage. And dustage. And no more Lucifentage.

I stare in horror as the one guy who knows how to stop me from changing into a vampire goes up in a pile of smoke.

But before I can mourn this fact properly, Big Bertha turns to us with an evil-looking metal-mouthed grin and I realize we may have bigger problems on our hands.

Crap.

"Run!" Magnus cries.

I don't need a second invitation.

We dash down the hall, Bertha hot on our heels. Magnus yanks me into a side chamber and slams the door shut, jamming a chair under the handle. My heart slams against my rib cage as I watch him run to the bookcase on the far side of the room and start scanning it with his eyes.

What is he doing?

I can hear Bertha pounding on the door.

"This is no time for book club!" I exclaim.

Magnus ignores me and pulls out a large, dusty tome from the shelf. Suddenly the bookshelf swings open, revealing a secret passageway leading off into the darkness.

Oh. My bad.

"Hurry," he hisses.

Behind us, Bertha's now hacking at the door with what sounds like an axe. Which is weird 'cause she didn't have an axe on her, just a stake. But I'm not going to ask questions.

I follow Magnus down into the dark tunnel and the bookshelf swings shut, blanketing us in complete darkness. The vampire grabs hold of my hand and starts dragging me down the stairs.

I can't see a thing and my heart is still pounding in my chest. I can't believe that slayer chick just dusted the three-thousand-year-old leader of the vampires in one fell swoop.

Dusted him seconds before he could tell me how to avoid becoming a three-thousand-year-old vampire myself.

And now she's after us. Which means I may no longer need to know the 411 on stopping the transformation, mainly due to the fact that I'll be reduced to a pile of gray dust way before it takes place. Instamatic cremation.

Will my life ever be normal again?

10

Confessions of a Teenage Knight in Shining Armor

We reach what appears to be a steel door, illuminated by a single torch. Magnus pulls it open and grabs the torch. We enter a tiny room, about the size of an elevator, with no furniture. The vampire locates a keypad panel and presses in a code. The door clangs shut.

Letting out a sigh of relief, Magnus affixes his torch to a bracket on the wall and slumps down to the floor. I join him.

"Are you okay?" he asks, turning to look at me. He's still breathing heavily.

"Yeah, I'm fine," I say, for some reason a bit touched by his concern. After all, he just watched his three-thousand-year-old boss go up in a pile of dust. Probably pretty darn traumatic for the guy. And still, he's worried about how I'm doing.

"That was far too close," he says, still breathing in ragged puffs. "I can't believe she got Lucifent."

"No kidding," I say. I look around the room. It appears to be made completely of some kind of slick, shiny metal. "What is this place?"

"It's a safe room," Magnus explains. "There are a few feet of solid titanium separating us from the rest of the compound. She'll never get in here. We just have to wait it out. She'll leave eventually. After all, she's got school in the morning."

"So let me get this straight," I say, pulling my knees to my chest and trying to still my heart. "That chick was a vampire slayer?"

"Indeed," Magnus says, "Every generation there is born a girl destined to slay all the vampires, rid the world of evil, yada, yada, yada." He shakes his head. "Which is absolutely ridiculous. We're not evil. We don't even kill humans anymore. We keep to ourselves, donate millions to charity, the works."

Interesting. "But the slayers don't buy this, I take it?"

"Please," he snorts. "A few years back, we launched this whole PR campaign. *Vamps Are People Too,* we called it. We sent the parent company, Slayer Inc., press releases, Quick-Time movies highlighting some of the more philanthropic among our ranks, everything. But did that convince them? No. They refused to listen. Insisted it was their *destiny*, whatever the bloody hell that means. It doesn't matter to Slayer Inc. that some of the greatest artists and musicians of our time are vampires. That they are killing off valuable members of society who would never hurt a fly."

"Ooh, musicians? Like who? Marilyn Manson? The guy from Nine Inch Nails? Green Day?" Ooh, I hope Billie Joe is a vamp. Then maybe I'll get to meet him. Maybe he even lives right here in the coven. You know, with riches and rock stars, I gotta admit there may be SOME good things about being a vampire.

"Their identities are secret," Magnus, the spoilsport, explains. "I could tell you, but then I'd have to kill you."

"Technically aren't I already dead?" I ask with a smile, remembering our previous conversation.

"Once again, you fail to grasp the concept of 'figure of speech.'"

"Yeah, yeah. So who are the musicians?"

He groans. "You're like a pit bull with a bone, aren't you?"

I grin proudly.

"Well, you've seen *Behind the Music* on VH1, right? Rockumentaries on gifted musicians who are always dying young in the second half hour?"

"'When we come back, the tragedy that shook their world,'" I quote with a giggle.

"Um, right." Magnus says, rolling his eyes. "Well, do you honestly think every one of these stars just had really bad luck in the tragic accident department?"

Hmm. I never really thought about it that way before. I'd always attributed the multitude of rocker deaths to the live fast, die young, leave a good-looking corpse, James Dean theory of life. But could it be that they were already rocking out as good-looking corpses, only to be killed a second time by a destiny-deluded Slayer with no appreciation for rock-'n'-roll?

You know, if I get out of this, I should write a tell-all book about the vampire world. Maybe I could get on *Oprah*. Or at the least *The Daily Show* . . .

"Do you remember that program that used to be on TV?" Magnus continues. "The one about the Slayer? That sympathizer Joss Whedon wrote the character to be so noble and good. Always saving the world from this vampire or that demon. But it's not like that in real life. The real-life Slayer is a vindictive ugly bitch with no compassion." He stares up at the dark ceiling. "And now she's killed Lucifent. This is a sad day for vampire kind indeed."

"For Sunny kind, as well," I add, frowning. "Seeing as he was just about to tell me how I could reverse the whole vampire transformation thing. Does this mean I'm going to be stuck as a bloodsucker for eternity? Or until I get dusted by some Slayer?"

Magnus shrugs. "Maybe not," he says. "Lucifent has a whole library of ancient texts. Certainly one of them will have the answer. Once we get out of here, we can take a look."

Okay, that makes me feel a tad better. Maybe there's hope after all.

"Oh, Lucifent," Magnus moans suddenly, banging the back of his head against the titanium wall. That's gotta hurt, even for a vamp. "Why did it have to be you?"

"You seem awfully upset about a guy who was screaming and calling you mean names just a minute ago," I venture, not quite sure how to react to this sudden display of emotion.

Magnus turns to look at me, his eyes filled with bloody tears, which is kind of gross, actually. I wonder if he sweats blood, too. That sure would make for some interesting gym habits.

"Lucifent was my sire," he explains in a slow voice. "My original blood mate, though we didn't call them that back then. He was the one to turn me into a vampire."

"Ah." It's starting to make sense now. I feel an unwilling pang of pity for poor Magnus. Seeing Lucifent, his vampire daddy, go up in a puff of smoke must be pretty traumatizing for the guy. In fact, I'm amazed he had the wherewithal to make sure I got out alive as well.

"So why did you want to become a vampire?" I ask curiously. "Was it the riches and power, like Rayne wants?"

Magnus shakes his head. "Hardly," he says. "Things were a lot different back when I was turned."

He straightens his legs out along the floor and stretches his hands above his head in a yawn. I refuse to notice how this stretched-out position accentuates his washboard abs. Nope, they're not even a blip on my radar.

"Different how?"

"It's a long story, actually."

I shrug. "We've got nothing but time."

"Too right." He grins, ruefully. "Well, it all started about a thousand years ago. When I served as one of King Arthur's Knights of the Round Table."

I do a double take. "King Arthur? So he really did exist?"

Magnus scowls and gives me one of his famous 'are you kidding me, you babe in the woods?' looks. "Of *course* he existed," he says, with mondo indignation.

"Oh. Okay. But I thought—"

"Uh, up until yesterday you also thought there was no such thing as vampires."

He has a point there.

"So you worked for the guy? Sat at the Round Table? Hung out in Camelot?" I try to picture Magnus in shining armor instead of his typical shining Armani. I bet he was pretty sexy as a knight. All the damsels probably went crazy over him. I wonder if he had a wife. Kids. Ugh. Why does the thought of him having kids scar me so much? I mean, who cares? So he had a life a thousand years before I was born. Big whoop.

"Did you know Lancelot?" I ask, to get my mind off the scarring kids thing.

"Lancelot," Magnus snorts disgustedly. "Why is it that everyone always asks about that pansy? I just love how all the legends have been twisted to make him seem like some kind of hero. The guy hardly ever showed up to fight. He was too busy shagging Queen Guinevere behind the king's back. I mean, thanks to him, poor Arthur lost his throne and Camelot was destroyed. So yeah," he says, sarcastically. "Not my favorite person, let me tell you."

There goes one childhood fantasy flushed down the toilet.

"Never mind about Lancelot. How did you get turned into a vampire? Was it by Merlin? The Lady of the Lake? Ooh, I know. Morgan le Fay, the witch. She did it, right?" I'd paid attention in our Arthurian legends unit in history class last year. The stories were too juicy to resist.

"As I was saying," Magnus continues, ignoring my guesses, "we knights were sent to the eastern lands on a crusade. Our mission was to convert the pagans and, more importantly, find the Holy Grail." He turns to look at me. "That's the cup that Jesus Christ used during the Last Supper."

"I know what it is. I'm not stupid," I say. "I mean, I've seen *Indiana Jones and the Last Crusade*. And Monty Python, of course."

Magnus screws up his face. "Um, right. Well, in any case, not long after we arrived, our order was captured by the Moors in the city of Bethlehem. We were thrown into prison. Beaten and starved until we were very close to death. I thought my life would end in that prison. End at age eighteen." Magnus pauses, then adds, "But really, that's where it all began."

I nod. "Okay, go on." This is getting to be a darn good story. For a moment, I almost forget I'm stuck in a deep, dark, underground titanium room with only a vampire to keep me company.

"Back then vampires didn't have donor blood banks like we do today. So in order to get the blood they needed to survive, they were forced to suck it from the necks of unwilling humans. Very un-PC, I know, but what can you do? It was a barbaric age all around. Anyway, one night, Lucifent arrived at the Moorish prison to search for victims. When he saw the torture we prisoners had endured, he was horrified. He couldn't believe such cruelty existed."

"And this from a man who ripped open throats on a nightly basis."

Magnus frowns. "He did it in the most humane manner possible," he insists, shooting me a glare.

"Okay, okay. I'll stop ragging on your sire. Jeez," I say, a bit sulkily.

Magnus shakes his head, then continues. "So, in an act of raw passion, Lucifent murdered all the guards, draining *their* blood instead of ours for his midnight snack. They didn't even see him coming. Then, when he was done, he set us all free."

"Well that was awfully nice of him," I say, trying to earn back my brownie points.

"But I was too weak to get away," Magnus explains. "My muscles had atrophied from nearly a year's imprisonment and I couldn't get up. So Lucifent asked me if I would like to die, or if I'd prefer eternal life." Magnus shrugs. "You can probably guess what I chose."

"Wow. That's some story!" I say, impressed. I try to imagine what it'd be like to live in the twelfth century. To go on crusades and be captured, tortured, with no Geneva Convention to stop them from doing their worst. "So you've been a vampire ever since?"

"Yes. Through the rise of the British Empire, the founding of America, the Industrial Revolution, the Civil War. Through the Roaring Twenties and the Great Depression. World War I, World War II. Kennedy to Khrushchev. Disco and techno. The Electric Slide and the Boot Scootin' Boogie. All of J-Lo's marriages and P. Diddy's name changes. You name it, I've lived through it."

"And are you happy? Do you like being a vampire?"

Magnus is silent for a moment. "In a way," he says at last. "Eternal life is a great gift. I've had so many adventures. So many experiences. At the same time, it's a bit . . . lonely."

"Lonely?"

"All my mortal friends have been dead a thousand years," he says softly, staring at the ground. "And until you're matched with your blood mate, which doesn't happen till you hit the millennium mark and your blood is properly aged, you're not really supposed to get into any serious relationships."

Wow. This guy hasn't had a date in a thousand years? No wonder he's so cranky!

"And now, just my luck, I'd finally been approved for a blood mate. A partner I'm allowed to love and care for and spend the rest of eternity with. And then I go and screw up royally and bite the wrong girl." He slams a fist against the floor. "Now I'll probably be doomed to walk the earth alone for the rest of my life."

I study him sympathetically. Poor guy. All he wanted was a nice girlfriend who appreciated him. Instead he got saddled with whiny, unappreciative me.

"No offense to you and all," he adds, looking up at me, his eyes sad. "You're a sweet girl. But obviously you have no interest in being my companion. And to tell you the truth, I'd rather have no blood mate than one who abhors me and thinks I'm some kind of monster."

A pang of guilt stabs at my gut. This whole time I've been nothing but selfish. Thinking only of myself and what a pain this whole vampire mix-up has been for me. I never considered how much it's probably screwed him up as well. Here he was, finally getting the blood mate he's been waiting a millennium for. A willing partner to share eternity with. (Even if it was just my silly twin sister.) And now everything's all screwed up.

"So do you love Rayne?" I ask curiously, wondering how much of a bond pre–blood mates share.

Magnus shakes his head. "I barely know her. You're not allowed that much contact before the actual transformation. It's sort of like how they used to do arranged marriages back in the old days. The Council decides on your blood mate based on some very complex compatibility algorithms. After all, once you're mated, you're stuck together for eternity, so it's something they take pretty seriously."

"And they thought you and Rayne would be a good fit?"

"Evidently. And I think they were probably right. I met her a few times during the training and she seems like a brilliant girl. And call me a shallow male—" he adds with a grin "—but she's obviously very beautiful as well."

I can feel myself blushing down to my toes. If he thinks Rayne is beautiful, that means he thinks I'm beautiful by default, seeing as we're identical and all. Not that I care what he thinks. Really. After all, there's no reason to start getting all interested in this guy. I need to concentrate on finding a way to turn back to a human, not finding excuses to flirt with a thousand-year-old vampire. Even if the vampire in question is an Orlando Bloom look-alike who used to serve King Arthur.

Besides, let's be frank here. Magnus is a royal pain in the butt. Annoying. Self-serving. The kind of guy who only thinks of himself and doesn't care about the needs of others.

"You look cold. Here, take my coat," Magnus says, pulling his leather jacket off and handing it to me. I reluctantly shrug it on.

Okay, maybe not self-centered. But definitely a jerk. Mean and arrogant.

"Don't worry, Sunny," he says, putting an arm around my shoulders and pulling me close to him. I grudgingly fold into his way-too-comfortable embrace. "I promise to find a way to turn you back. No matter what it takes."

Whoa. He's not making this easy for me, is he?

11

Garlic and Sunshine and Raw Meat—Oh My!

We remain in the titanium room for hours. I actually fall asleep for a short bit, waking up with my head on Magnus's shoulder, which is way embarrassing, let me tell you. I hope I didn't drool on him at any point.

Finally, after what seems an eternity of waiting, the computerized female voice announces that, just like Elvis, "The Slayer has left the building."

We exit the room and head back into the main coven. The place is deserted. Magnus explains that most of the vamps were already out feeding when the Slayer arrived and most likely don't yet realize that their fearless leader has been taken from them.

He leads me to the exit, telling me he's going to take me

home first, then return to research my reversal in the library. At first I suggest I help him read, but then he admits that he's planning on feeding in between taking me home and researching, which I decide I'm not ready to take part in. I mean, sure, I get the fact that his donors are willing and screened, but the idea of watching him drain them of blood just isn't what I'd call an entertaining nighttime outing. And anyway, Magnus promised he'll text-message me the second he finds something.

So I get home around five A.M. (The ride in the convertible Jag is heavenly, BTW!) I know I should be exhausted, but I'm wide awake. I tiptoe to my room, attempting not to wake up my mom, since I don't think she's going to buy the "I only missed curfew 'cause I was hiding out from a Vampire Slayer who killed Haley Joel Osment right before my very eyes" excuse.

Luckily she's a deep sleeper.

I arrive at my bedroom and switch on the light. My eyes fall on a figure asleep in my bed. Rayne. She must have tried to stay up waiting for me. I crawl into bed beside her and turn out the light. She rolls over with a soft moan.

"Oh," she murmurs. "I didn't realize you were home."

"Just got," I say, pulling the covers over me. After spending the night on a hard titanium floor, I find the bed's softness more than welcoming to my achy, tired body.

"So what happened? Did Lucifent turn you back? Are you a human again?"

I sigh. "No. He was about to tell us how to reverse the process. Said it was simple and everything. But then he got dusted by the Slayer."

Rayne sits up in bed. Even in the predawn darkness I can see her wide eyes. "The Slayer?"

"Yeah, once a generation there's evidently some girl who's destined to kill vampires or something like that. Like in Buffy."

"I know what the Slayer is," Rayne says impatiently. "I just can't believe she got Lucifent! That's terrible. Such a great loss for vampire kind worldwide."

"I don't know." I shrug. "He seemed like kind of an asshole to me."

"Sunny, Lucifent has done so much for the coven. You don't even know. If you'd read my blog—"

"Will you shut up about the blog already?" I know I'm being bitchy, but you'd be too if you'd spent your night the way I had.

Rayne lies back down in bed. "I can't believe Lucifent's dead," she mutters, staring up at the ceiling. When we were kids we pasted glow-in-the-dark stars all over it and some of them are still glowing—tiny pinpricks of green light. Such innocent times, then.

"*I* can't believe I may be stuck as a vampire forever," I retort. Jeez. Enough with the feeling-sorry-for-Lucifent thing already. Sunny needs pity, too. "I mean, this is going to put a serious damper on my social life. Not to mention my high school career."

My voice cracks on the last sentence. Damn it, I don't want to cry again. But I'm tired and stressed and afraid and I just can't seem to help it. Once I let one tear escape, the rest start catapulting down my face like a freaking waterfall.

"I don't want to be a . . . a vampire," I choke out.

Rayne rolls on her side and brushes a lock of hair off my forehead, studying me with concerned eyes. "I'm sorry, sweetie," she says. "I keep forgetting how hard this must be for you." She kisses me on the cheek, then starts climbing out of bed. "I'll let you get some sleep."

"Can't you stay?" I ask, the words leaving my mouth before I can stop them. She's going to think I'm such a baby, but suddenly I don't want to be alone anymore. Alone with my tormented thoughts.

She nods and gets back into bed, no questions asked. "Sure," she says, squirming into a more comfortable position. "What are twin sisters for?"

The DJ responsible for the music playing on my clock radio should be shot. No, that wouldn't be painful enough. He should be castrated and left to be eaten by rabid dogs. Or something. "The Monster Mash" is my morning wake-up song—puh-leeze. Inhuman, I tell you.

I press the snooze bar and pull the covers over my head. I've never felt so exhausted in all my life. I feel like I'm going to throw up, I'm so tired. I don't think I even got to sleep before the sun was peeking over the horizon. And then, I fell into an almost coma-deep slumber until the DJ decided to torment me with this cruel and unusual musical punishment.

But Rayne, the suddenly evil bee-yotch who's probably in cahoots with the DJ, isn't content to let me sleep. She shakes me by the shoulder. "Wake up, Sun," she commands in an overly chipper voice. So help me, if she breaks into the "Good Morning" song my mother used to sing to get us up when we were kids, I won't be held responsible for my actions. "We've got to go to school."

"I'm sick," I mumble, resisting her shakes.

"You're not sick. You're just a vampire," she clarifies, as if that makes everything okay. "So it makes sense you want to sleep through the day."

Her words make me bolt upright in bed. OMG, she's right! I *am* acting like a vampire. I stayed up all night and now I'm hoping to sleep all day. Ugh. I don't want to succumb to these vamp urges. For all I know, it might make it more difficult to reverse the transformation if I'm all accepting of it and stuff.

"I'm up," I say, rubbing my eyes. The sunlight streaming through the window feels like fire on my skin. I think I'll be using the 30 SPF this morning. Or maybe the turbocharged 50+ stuff Mom keeps in her bathroom.

I sniff the air. "Ugh. What's that awful smell?" I ask, screwing up my nose.

Rayne shrugs. "Smells like Mom's making breakfast."

"That sure doesn't smell like any breakfast I'd want to eat," I say, climbing out of bed and trying to dodge the scattered sunny parts of the room as I make my way to the bathroom.

I wash my face and notice I'm looking especially pale this A.M. Kind of like what Rayne looks like when she pancakes her face white for the extreme Goth look. Oh well, so much for getting a tan. I slather on the sunscreen, careful not to miss any pertinent parts, then head back into my bedroom. Rayne's left by this point, and I'm more than tempted to crawl back into bed. But no, I must resist the urge. I need to keep acting as normal as possible.

Besides, if I go to school I get to see Jake Wilder. The Jake Wilder who's wildly attracted to me. Talk about motivation!

I look in my closet for something to wear. Something that will impress Jake, preferably. Unfortunately, even though it's meant to hit like eighty today, I don't think my normal tank and flips are going to cut it in the wardrobe department. Too much risk for sunburn. Better to cover as much skin as possible.

So I choose a black sweater with bell sleeves that go over my hands, my favorite pair of Diesel jeans, and a pair of black boots. Now all that's exposed is my face and neck. (The bite mark has thankfully faded!) I grab a pair of dark sunglasses from my dresser and a worn Red Sox cap. I study myself in the mirror (yes, BTW, I *can* still see my reflection; guess that one was a myth), sort of feeling like a Hollywood celeb going undercover to grocery shop. Not exactly the best look to attract Jake, but hey, that's what the Vampire Scent is for, I guess.

Satisfied with my outfit, I clomp down the stairs, ready to face the world. Or at least my mother. But the putrid smell only gets worse as I approach the kitchen. Ew! What the hell is she cooking this time? Fried rotting rat?

Let me just say for the record here, my "yes, I went to Woodstock" mom has made some pretty odd recipes over the years. (Tofu manicotti, anyone?) So I can only imagine what she's cooked up this time around. (And BTW, the Woodstock thing? She neglects to mention that she was five years old at the time and spent more time running around naked in the mud, being chased by my exasperated grandma, than listening to the music. Then again, I guess a lot of adults were doing the same thing, so who am I to judge the cultural influence the event had on her existence?)

"Burning down the kitchen, Mom?" I joke as I enter the room. The smell is almost overwhelming now, and I have to take a step back to steady myself. It's a burnt, decomposing odor that makes me want to vomit. I pause for a moment, blinking my eyes a few times, as they've started watering like crazy.

"What's wrong, honey?" Mom asks, turning from whatever horror she's concocting, a concerned look on her face. "You look awful."

"I feel awful," I say, slumping into a kitchen chair, trying to resist the urge to plug my nose with my fingers. As bad as the smell is, it's obviously something she's slaved over and I can't be that rude. Just hope she doesn't expect me to eat any of it.

Mom wipes her hands on her apron and approaches me. She puts her palm against my forehead. "You don't feel sick," she says, wrinkling her brow. "In fact, your forehead is ice cold."

I pull my head away before she starts wondering about my perfectly chilled vampire temperature.

"What is that . . . smell?" I manage to choke out, wanting to change the subject.

She cocks her head in confusion. "Smell?" she asks. She sniffs the air. "All I can smell is the breakfast scramble I'm cooking up." She shrugs. "Tofu, peppers, and lots of garlic, just the way you like it."

Gah! Realization hits me over the head like a cartoon anvil. That's got to be it. I've suddenly developed the stereotypical vampire aversion to garlic. A food product I used to adore. Go figure.

"Here, it's ready, actually," she says, walking back over to the stove and heaping a mammoth portion onto a plate. "You want salt on it?"

What I want is for the whole thing to be thrown in the trash, honestly. Preferably the neighbor's trash. The neighbor who lives on planet Pluto. That might be far enough away for me to withstand the stench.

But what am I supposed to say? I wonder, as she carries the steaming plate o'puke over to the table. Mom knows it's my favorite and she made it especially for me. Maybe I can take one bite—

Oh no. I'm going to hurl.

I jump out of my seat and bolt to the bathroom. I barely make it to the toilet before my stomach releases all its contents into the porcelain bowl.

• Okay. It's decided. I'm definitely not eating the breakfast scramble. Mom's hurt feelings be damned.

"Sunny, are you okay in there?" Mom asks, knocking on the door and sounding even more concerned than she did before.

"She's fine." I can hear Rayne's voice outside the door. Thank goodness. She can cover for me while I brush the vomit out of my teeth.

"She's not fine, honey. She just threw up."

"She's just nervous. We have a huge history test today."

"Are you sure, Rayne?" Hmm. Mom sounds suspicious. I guess that makes sense. I mean for all her peace, love, and flower-child beliefs, she hasn't just fallen off the turnip truck either. She knows I'm an excellent test taker. It's Rayne who has the nervous test-taking fits that she believes exonerate her from going to school on exam day.

"She's right," I say, exiting the bathroom with a smile. "I'm fine, Mom. Just got the old butterflies. After all, this test counts as twenty-five percent of our grade."

"Okay. If you're sure . . ." Mom says, still looking doubtful. "But you know, Sunny, you'd probably feel more confident if you had stayed in and studied last night instead of going out. I didn't even hear you come in."

Shoot. I'd forgotten about that.

"I was over at a study partner's house," I say, crossing my fingers behind my back. "We were going over history and kind of lost track of time."

Okay, before you think I'm a horrible person for lying to my mom, technically I'm not fibbing whatsoever. I *was* at Magnus's "house" last night and we *were* talking about history. The history of King Arthur, the crusades, and vampires, to be exact. But since there really isn't any test to begin with, I think I'm owed some creative license over what I studied to pass it.

For a moment Mom looks like she doesn't buy my explanation. But then she shrugs. "Okay, sweetie. I'm glad you studied. I've got to get to work." She reaches over and kisses me on the forehead and then does the same to Rayne. "Have a good day, girls. And good luck on the test."

I watch as she heads to the front closet to retrieve her handbag. I feel bad lying to her. As far as moms go, she's pretty cool. Not like some of my friends' moms who act more like prison wardens than parents. She's always been the "Friend Mom." The one who promises she'll never judge us for telling her things. The type who'd rather we ask for condoms or birth control than go out and have sex without telling her. She's open and accepting and loving.

But I still don't think she'd get the whole vampire thing. After all, "Friend Mom" does not necessarily equal "Accept That Your Daughter Is Turning Undead and Be Cool with That Mom."

"Bye, girls," she says, waving as she exits.

"Bye, Mom," we chorus.

Now alone, Rayne and I let out nervous laughter.

"That was close," I say, heaving a sigh of relief.

"No kidding," Rayne agrees. "Though I do think she's still a bit suspicious."

"She probably thinks I'm pregnant and having morning sickness or something. Throwing up at the sight of food."

"Nah. She knows you better than that," Rayne says with a laugh. "My little Sunny the Innocent," she coos, tousling my hair.

"What-EVER," I say, making the W with my fingers.

Rayne smirks. "Now if it were *me* throwing up, we'd already be in the car on the way to the clinic."

"Yes, indeed, 'cause you are a skanky ho," I say gleefully. Rayne playfully punches me in the arm. She thinks it's funny, go figure.

"Actually *you're* the skanky ho this time around. The bitch who stole my blood mate," she replies with a laugh. "And speaking of, how was the oh-so-dreamy Magnus last night?"

11111111112

For some reason her question makes my face heat in a blush. Though judging from how fair my skin is now, it probably doesn't even register a dusty rose.

"He's fine," I say. "Upset about Lucifent, of course. I mean the guy was his sire and all."

"Lucifent was Magnus's sire?" Rayne says, raising an eyebrow.

I smile, happy to finally know something she doesn't. "Yup," I say, and relate an abbreviated version of the tale.

When I'm finished, Rayne releases a long, dramatic sigh. "Wow," she says dreamily. "My blood mate was a knight in shining armor. How cool is that?"

I shrug. "Yeah, he's actually an interesting guy when he's not being all arrogant and rude." I pause, then add, "Which is ninety-nine percent of the time." Don't want Rayne to get the idea that I'm developing some kind of affection for Magnus, since I'm so not. In fact, I think a change of subject is in order here. "Now go toss out that disgusting garlic concoction before I gag again."

"Okay. I'll take it outside." Rayne disappears into the kitchen, and moments later she and the smell exit the house and the air becomes relatively clear again.

As the smell fades, I realize I'm suddenly ravenously hungry. I enter the kitchen, searching for a garlic-free snack. I peer into the fridge. Not much there. Then my eyes fall on a package of hamburger meat in the very back of the fridge.

My mom's a strict vegetarian, you see, and brought me up that way as well. But my sister could never lose her taste for red meat. So once in a while she gives in to her carnivorous urges and enjoys a good burger.

I stare at the hamburger, suddenly realizing my mouth is watering. In fact, I'm suddenly craving it so badly that I think I might be drooling a bit.

Suddenly, my hand reaches involuntarily to the raw meat, as if it's taken on a will of its own. My stomach growls in anticipation. It looks so luscious. So red. So delicious.

I look around to see if Rayne's back. She's probably still burying the garlic mess. I have time. I grab the package and tear it open, greedily grabbing handfuls of raw meat and shoveling them into my mouth, rejoicing in the bloody juices flowing down my throat. I swear, a chocolate peanut-butter sundae with extra whipped cream and chocolate sauce could not taste half this good.

"You know that's a real good way to develop *E. coli.*"

I whirl around, mouth full of raw meat, to see Rayne standing there with a smirk on her face. I suddenly realize what I'm doing. Horrified, I spit the meat out into the sink, trying to force myself to throw the rest up.

"Oh my God. I can't believe I just did that," I cry, absolutely mortified. "That's so disgusting."

"It's okay. I'm sure vampires are immune to food-borne illness," Rayne says.

"But it's so . . . gross!" I stare at the rest of the beef, fighting the nearly overwhelming urge to dig back in. "I can't believe I just ate raw hamburger. It's all bloody and slimy and—"

"Don't beat yourself up over it, Sun. You're just giving in to your vampire urges, is all." Rayne shrugs. "Pretty soon you'll have to be moving on to live blood, though."

I narrow my eyes. "I am sooo not partaking of live blood."

"You will if you're hungry enough."

"No. I won't. I definitely won't. Cross my heart, hope to die. I vow on my prom date with Jake Wilder," I promise. "I will never, ever be that hungry."

My stomach growls in response. Uh-oh.

12

Roses Are Red,
Blood Is Too . . .

"Sunshine McDonald, please report to the principal's office."

I perk up out of my sleep-deprived coma at my name being called over the loudspeaker system. I'm in trig class, which I hate, and have been hiding out in the back row, head in my hands, trying to do the whole "look awake while sleeping" pose.

I'm so tired. So, so tired. I don't know how I'm going to get through this week, let alone the rest of my existence. If Magnus doesn't find a vampire antidote, I'm doomed to be a high school dropout.

I glance over at the teacher to make sure he's heard the announcement. He must have, as he simply waves me toward the door with a saucy smile. Ew. He's like the fifth male teacher today to flirt with me. This Vampire Scent thing is great for boys my age, like Jake, but when it starts affecting pervert adults it gets a little freaky.

I rise from my seat, thanking Lover Boy with a nod, and he goes back to calculating huge incomprehensible math problems on the board with a big goofy grin on his face. Major ew-age.

I'm happy to step into the hallway, away from class, but I soon realize this might be going from the frying pan to the fire. I have no idea why I'm being summoned to the principal's office, but usually that sort of thing is never good. Then again, I've done nothing wrong. I haven't said or done anything weird, I haven't bitten any of the student body. I did run out of home ec class after the teacher announced we were going to bake cheesy garlic bread, but I later blamed that on my aversion to carbs due to my South Beach Diet.

I arrive at the glassed-in office and step inside, my heart beating furiously. I so don't need to get in trouble on top of everything else.

"Hi, I'm Sunshine McDonald," I say to Miss Rose, the longtime school secretary sitting at the front desk. "You guys called me?"

Miss Rose looks up. She's an older woman, probably in her sixties, wearing a prim little pastel suit with a perfect string of pearls. Got the Barbara Bush look down pat.

But when she sees me, her demure smile morphs into what looks like a lecherous grin.

"Hi, sweetie," she purrs in a low, sensual voice that no Barbara Bush look-alike should ever be allowed to use. "I'm so glad you could come down." She gives me the once-over from head to toe. "You're looking awfully pretty today, dear."

I take a step back, a little shaken. Has she been affected by the Vampire Scent? She couldn't be! It only works on guys and . . .

I start to laugh. I can't help it. The whole thing is just so absurd. So surreal. I can't believe I'm in school being hit on by a secretly lesbian grandma.

Miss Rose frowns at my merriment, looking rather offended. Poor thing.

"Sorry," I say, swallowing hard to contain my chortling. "The principal wanted to see me?"

"No, dear," Miss Rose says in wounded tone. "I had them page you so you could pick up your flowers."

"Flowers?"

Miss Rose gestures to the desk adjacent to hers. My eyes fall on an absolutely enormous bouquet of blood-red roses. There must be at leave five dozen in the vase, all meticulously arranged by some expert florist.

"For me?" I ask, mentally cataloging my brain for who could have possibly sent me roses.

And delightfully, the only person I can think of is Jake Wilder.

Of course. It makes perfect sense. He can't stop thinking about me and our prom date on Saturday night. He wants to thank me for saying yes with this "little" token of his appreciation. Something to hold me over until he brings me my corsage. .

I walk over to the flowers and breathe through my nose, taking in their soft, powdery scent. Jake's such a wonderful guy. So thoughtful. So sweet. I reach for the card, hardly able to wait to read what I'm sure will be cleverly written poetry, professing his undying love for—

Damn it, the flowers are from Magnus.

I stare at the card, at first so lost in my fantasy world that I think maybe the florist just delivered the wrong bouquet. But no, the card says my name. It's just signed by a vampire instead of my prom date.

So disappointing.

I glance over at the flowers. He probably freaking stole them from the graveyard or something. Jerk. Why would he send me flowers anyway?

I glance at the card again.

Dear Sunny,
I'm so sorry for all you've had to go through due to my dreadful mistake. I'm sure last night was especially

traumatic for you. Please accept this tiny token of my apology and meet me at Club Fang tonight, to discuss your situation.

Yours truly,

Magnus

I release an exasperated sigh. Now I have to go back to Club Fang? I'm already way behind on my homework, having gone out the past two nights. You know, turning into a vampire is bad enough without me flunking out of school as well.

But what choice do I have? If I want to reverse this process, I've got to do what he says.

"Sunny, dearest, would you like to come and sit on Miss Rose's lap?" the secretary invites, while fluttering her white eyelashes. "I've been dying to talk to you."

Ugh. That settles it. Club Fang, here I come!

13

The Donor Chicks

I arrive at Club Fang at around eight P.M. Unlike last Sunday, tonight there's no DJ in a bondage cage and no one's doing the foot-stuck-in-the-mud dance to suicide-inducing music. No, tonight, the club's been transformed into a hip-looking coffeehouse and wine bar, with its inhabitants lounging at various café tables, looking trendily bored as they suck down frothy cappuccinos and glasses of wine.

I check a few of them out, trying to decide which are the vampires and which are the humans who love them. Since everyone's pale faced, red lipped, and dressed uniformly in black, it's surprisingly hard to tell the creatures of the night from those still among the living.

I see Magnus at the back of the room, sitting at a small table, accompanied by two hot girls. He catches my eye and motions me over. I realize I'm strangely excited to see him, which is very annoying, since that's not the kind of power I want him to have over me.

It's probably just the anticipation of me turning back into a human that's got my heart beating faster and my breath catching in my throat, I remind myself. It's not like Magnus turns me on in any way, shape, or form, that's for sure. Especially, I note, as I get closer, not in that outfit. I mean, who would get turned on by a fitted black T-shirt that perfectly molds itself to his sculpted six-pack abs or a pair of tight black leather pants that showcases—

Okay. Fine. I admit it, I'm attracted. Very attracted. In fact, I'm willing to bet I'm more attracted to this vampire hottie than I am to Robert Pattinson, Chace Crawford, and Brad Pitt put together. So sue me.

Bottom line, attraction does not equal wanting to remain someone's blood mate for all of eternity. Period. End o' story.

As I reach the table, the two girls, pierced and tattooed out to the max, look up and stare at me with unfriendly, black-rimmed eyes. Oh, let me guess, more jealous Magnus disciples, hating me 'cause I'm the guy's blood mate. As if I signed up for the stupid gig.

"Hi," I say, looking straight at Magnus and ignoring his groupies. The guy should consider becoming a rock star like the vampire Lestat did in that Anne Rice book *Queen of the Damned*. He'd probably do very well in the screaming teenage fans department.

"Hey," Magnus greets back, glancing at the girls with a smug smile, looking oh-so-proud of himself. I frown. Does he expect me to be jealous of his fan club or something? Puh-leeze.

"Um . . ." I shuffle from foot to foot. Should I sit down? There's no extra chair.

"Sit," Magnus suddenly instructs, almost as if he's read my mind. OMG, he can't do that, can he? That would royally suck. Especially since I was just thinking about how sexy he is in that outfit.

Trying to shield my mind and think random non-Magnus thoughts about Marc Jacobs shoes and the square root of pi, just in case he does have some kind of mind-reading abilities, I grab a chair from a nearby table and take my seat.

"Um, hi, I'm Sunny," I say to the girl on my left. "Nice to meet you," I add, holding out my hand to the one on the right. "Do you guys come here often?"

The girl stares at my hand, but doesn't take it. She also doesn't answer my question.

What's her problem? Is she a mute or something? Or just incredibly rude? (Judging from whom I've met so far in the vamp community, I'm betting on the latter.)

"It's okay, Rachel. You can talk to her," Magnus says, oh-so-grandly giving his permission. Jeez. He really does get off on this all-powerful-vampire thing, doesn't he?

Then again, people let him get away with it. Like this Rachel chick, for instance. I mean, Magnus commands and both girls suddenly light up like those animatronic characters at Disney World. What's up with that? Are they trapped under some kind of Magnus mind control or something? Or are they just your typical obsessive Goths, like my sister, willing to do whatever the big bad vamps command?

"Greetings, oh honored one. I am Rachel," says the girl on my left in a reverential, way overly dramatic tone. "And this is my companion, Charity."

"Hiya, Sunny," says Charity, in a surprisingly squeaky valley-girl voice. Wow. I hadn't expected that to come from her blood-red-lipped mouth. "We've, like, heard so much about you."

They have? They've heard about me? That would mean Magnus talks about me. Talks about me to his friends even. Which is interesting, of course, but certainly no reason to have my heart start beating like crazy.

Trying to regain control of my once-again traitorous body, I study the girls more closely. Both have long, impossibly straight black hair, soft blue eyes, and china doll skin. Hmm . . . I wonder . . .

"Are you guys . . . ?" I trail off, not quite sure of the PC terminology. Would a vampire be considered mortally challenged? "Are you . . . ?"

"Vampires?" Rachel fills in.

My face heats. "Uh, yeah." Okay, guess they're cool with the V-word here.

"No." Rachel says, shaking her head. "Unlike you, we are regretfully still attached to this mortal coil."

"We wish, though," Charity chimes in. "That would so totally rock if we were."

"Indeed," her friend agrees, solemnly. "To be a creature of the night would, as my dear friend so eloquently puts it, totally rock."

O-kay, so they're not vampires. But they know about vampires. They're like vamp wanna-bes. Maybe they're part of the training program Rayne was in?

"Actually, we're Donor Chicks," Charity informs me.

"Donor—?" I scrunch my eyebrows. Then realization hits me like a ten-ton truck. I stare from one to the other. "*You're* Magnus's blood donors?"

Wow. Magnus had told me that vampires contracted willing humans to provide them with their blood supply, but I didn't think about the fact that these donors would be very attractive young women. Dinner for Mag boy must be a real gourmet treat.

"Yes." Rachel nods enthusiastically. "We are bound to serve Lord Magnus," she says, smiling over at the vampire in question, looking prouder than a peacock. "Offer him our blood sacrifice so that he may sustain immortal life."

I roll my eyes. What a drama queen. "So what you're saying is you, like, willingly let him suck your blood? Why the heck would you sign up for something like that?" I'm trying not to be judgmental here, but seriously!

"Are you kidding?" Rachel frowns, her expression telling me that I've just asked the stupidest question known to humankind. "It is an honor to provide sustenance to such a powerful being," she explains. "By doing so, we too are indirectly taking part in immortal life."

"Plus it's great pay!" Charity interjects. Rachel shoots her an evil look, like it's rude to bring up the more mercenary aspects of their agreement.

But Charity ignores her. "I mean, for a young mom like myself, there's no better way to earn a few extra bucks on the side. Definitely beats waitressing for a living. Now I can take care of my baby, rent a kick-ass apartment, and have enough money to go to college. All without food stamps. It's a total win-win, you know? Maggy here gets his bloody-wuddy," she says, clucking a frowning Magnus under the chin, "and me and my baby get a big fat bank account."

Okay, then. There you have it. I mean, what can I possibly say to properly respond to that little spiel?

"Well, um, I'm glad it's all working out for you," I respond lamely. "Wouldn't be my first career choice, but hey, neither is astrophysics and plenty of people do that for a living and make out real well."

"Girls, could you get Sunny a drink?" Magnus says, speaking up for the first time. "She must be very thirsty."

Without even a pause to question why I can't get up and get my own damn drink, or why both of them have to go for that matter, the Donor Chicks jump up and head for the coffee bar.

"They're, um, cute," I remark, watching them across the room. Charity is giggling about something and Rachel is rolling her eyes at her.

Magnus shrugs. "They're dinner," he says simply. As if he's talking about a pork chop or something.

"They're also human," I protest, not knowing why I feel the need to defend them. After all, they certainly aren't unwilling victims. If they're stupid enough to think that the concept of a vampire downing their blood like some vintage red wine is cool, then who am I to say they're being exploited and used? "I mean, I knew you had donors, but it's just completely weird to meet them in person."

"I can imagine," Magnus says, twirling his wineglass in his hands. "I debated bringing them with me. I don't usually dine out."

Dine out. Hardy har har. "Is that supposed to be a lame attempt at a vampire joke?"

He smiles. "Pun was intended, yes." He takes a sip of his wine. "I usually swing by their houses early in the evening, then go on with my night."

"Ah. A bloody booty call." See, I can make vampire jokes too. "So no fraternizing with dinner allowed, then?"

"It's not against the rules," Magnus says with a shrug.

"We are allowed to associate with our donors if we choose to. In fact, I've heard of many donor-vamp relationships developing and lasting for years. But my particular donors are, how do I put this?" he asks, glancing over at the giggling girls. "A bit overwhelming at times."

"I see." Well, I guess that means he's not attracted to them. That's a relief . . . or not. Actually not. In fact, for the record, I think it'd be totally fine if he were attracted to them. If he had a relationship with them, even. Because after all, I couldn't care less who he's dating.

No, really.

"So why did you bring them here tonight?" I ask.

He grins. "For you. I thought you might like a bite to eat."

"Ha, ha. Very funny."

"I wasn't making a joke this time."

I screw up my face. "Ew! I'm *not* drinking anyone's blood." Then I blush as I remember the incident with the raw meat in the kitchen this morning. I really hope he can't read my mind, 'cause that was way embarrassing.

"You *have* to drink blood. You're a vampire."

"No. I don't have to and I won't. I'll just order a burger if I get hungry."

"A burger won't—"

"An extra-rare burger with lots of blood."

Magnus shakes his head. "A burger is all empty calories," he says. "You need to be nourished with human blood."

"I am not drinking blood. End of story."

"You should just try it. You'd probably like it."

"I won't like it. I know I won't."

"You probably didn't think you'd like brussels sprouts the first time you tried them either," he reasons.

"I still don't like brussels sprouts, just FYI. And I certainly will never, ever, in a million years like the taste of human blood."

Before Magnus can respond with some other idiotic reason why I should partake in this cannibalistic behavior, the Donor Chicks return, carrying a goblet of red wine.

Saved by the Goths.

"Here you go," says Charity, thrusting the drink at me. "Your merlot."

I take a sniff. It smells delicious. Not that I'm some wino, but this particular brand has a warm, spicy smell. I shouldn't be drinking wine. Especially not on a school night. Mom would absolutely kill me if she found out. But then again, I'm already dead, right? (See, I'm good at this vampire humor thing!)

I take a sip.

Mmmm. Thick and hearty. must be a very good vintage.

I take another sip. This is good stuff. Really satisfying. Warms my stomach almost immediately, washing away all the stress and frustrations of the day.

On my third sip, I look around the room. Funny, I would have totally guessed that a makeshift coffeehouse like this would serve only the cheap stuff. Like blush from a box or something.

Um, in fact, now that I think about it, why would a coffee-house serve wine at all? Would they even have a liquor license?

Then it hits me.

Oh.

My.

God.

I spit my mouthful of "wine" back in the glass, my stomach heaving in disgust. I feel like I'm going to be sick. I look up at Magnus, who is smiling smugly from across the table. It takes every ounce of willpower not to slug him one.

"You tricked me!" I cry. "This is blood, not wine, isn't it?"

"I knew you would like it," he says simply.

"You told me it was merlot," I accuse Charity.

She grins. "Lord Magnus asks that we call it that. It sounds more . . . civilized," she says with a giggle. "And, like, if you're out in public, you can't be talking about drinking the B-word 'cause people will lock you up and throw away the key."

I feel a little like locking myself up and throwing away the key at this very moment. I can't believe I just drank some random Goth girl's blood.

I can't believe I liked it.

I can't believe I'm staring at the glass, wanting to take another sip.

"Ugh. What's happening to me?" I moan.

"Look, Sunny," Magnus says, leaning over the table and meeting my eyes with his own deep, soulless ones. "You'd find things a lot easier if you'd just start embracing your inner vampire."

"But I don't want to be a vampire!"

He sighs. "You've made that exceedingly clear, believe me. However, until we manage to stop your transformation, by all accounts you *are* becoming a vampire. Therefore, you must do the things that vampires do. And if you do not drink blood, you will very simply waste away and die before you get the opportunity to change back."

Okay, I guess he has a point. I glance around the coffee-house, making sure no one's watching me, then take a tentative sip of the blood in my wineglass. Soon, I'm gulping it down with wild abandon. Gross, I know. But I can't seem to help it. It just tastes so yummy.

"Very good," Magnus says, as if praising a one-year-old for eating her first Cheerios.

"Yeah, yeah," I mumble between gulps. "Whatever I have to do." I am so not admitting how delicious I find the drink or how I'm dying for a second glass.

"Thank you, ladies," Magnus says, turning to the Donor Chicks. He pulls out a wallet from his back pocket and hands each a wad of cash. Guess vamp blood payment is an under-the-table type gig. "You are free to go."

They take the money and giggle once again as they kiss Magnus on each cheek.

"Thanks, Maggy," says Charity. "You're the best."

"I will see thee tomorrow evening," Rachel adds. "Till next time, my divine immortal one."

Oh, puh-leeze. This girl makes Rayne seem normal.

Without further ado, the girls wave good-bye to me and exit the coffeehouse. Magnus watches them go, then turns to me.

"Like I said . . ."

". . . a little overwhelming," I finish, nodding. "I totally see your point."

"So," Magnus says, clearing his throat. "I've done some research."

I lean forward in my chair, excited. "And?"

He pauses. "Do you want the good news or the bad news?"

Why do people always ask that? It only prolongs the suspense, don't you think? And really, what difference does it make which one you bring up first?

"The good news, I guess." After all, if I know the good news, then I'll be in a better mood to deal with the bad news.

"The good news is that according to the ancient texts I've researched, there is a way for the vampire transformation process to be reversed. A way for you to turn back into a human."

"Woot!" I cry, raising a fist in the air in triumph. That is good news! "I knew there had to be a way!"

Overjoyed, I can't resist the urge to lean across the table and give the surprised vampire a big smacking kiss on the cheek. "You rock, Magnus! Thanks so much! I knew you could do it."

He waves off my attempted embrace. "I haven't told you the bad news yet," he reminds me.

"Bring it on, then. No kind of bad news can wreck my day now."

"According to my research, the only way to turn you back into a human is to purify your blood. And the only substance I know of that can do this is a drop of blood from the Holy Grail."

The Holy Grail? Holy crap!

14

The Holy Freaking Grail?!

I stop celebrating, hands stuck in perpetual freeze-frame cabbage patch dance, and stare at Magnus.

"The Holy Grail?" I repeat, realizing my voice has risen to a screechy hiss. "The HOLY FREAKING GRAIL?"

Magnus dips his head in a nod. "I told you it was bad news."

"How the hell are we supposed to get a drop of blood from the Holy Grail? Does the Holy Grail even exist? I thought the Holy Grail was something that was made up by the Church . . . or Steven Spielberg." I slam my head against the table. "I'm doomed. Doomed, doomed, doomed. Doomed to walk the earth as a creature of the night forever. Doomed to drink ditsy donor blood for all eternity."

"Chill out, Sunny," Magnus commands, sounding a bit ticked off at my admittedly overdramatic display. "The Grail does exist. I've seen it with my own eyes."

I look up, hopeful once again. "You have?"

"Indeed."

"So then you know where it is?"

Magnus pauses. "Erm, not exactly."

I knew it! I just knew he'd say that. "DOOMED! I'M DOOMED!" I cry, commencing with further head-banging.

"Will you keep your voice down?" Magnus hisses. "You're upsetting the others."

I lift my head and look around. Sure enough, I've pretty much got the whole Club Fang giving me the evil eye.

"You know, not everyone sees being a vampire as a dooming prospect," scolds a black-caped, bleached-blond teen who looks alarmingly like Spike from the *Buffy* show. "In fact, some of us quite enjoy it."

Oh brother.

"Um, sorry?" I venture, deciding to go the humble, ignorant route. After all, come Saturday night I'm going to be one of the blood-drinkin' gang forever and ever, and I don't want to start off on the wrong foot. "I meant no offense. I'm sure it's a very pleasurable way to spend eternity and all. It's just, well, not really my cup of tea, you understand."

"Whatever," the Spike guy replies, turning back to his companions. "God, I hate vampire newbs!" he adds under his breath.

"So ANYWAY," Magnus interrupts loudly, before I can give "Spike" the finger, "I hadn't finished what I was going to say before you erupted into premature mourning."

"Oh. Sorry," I mutter. "Go on."

"As I was saying, the Holy Grail is not a myth. It's a real object of power. The cup was used by the Christ during his Last Supper, then retrieved by Joseph of Arimathea, who filled the cup with Jesus' blood after he died on the cross."

Filling a wineglass with the blood of the dead. Nice, normal guy, this Joseph of Arimathea. Then again, after just gulping down a goblet of *Château de Rachel et Charity*, I realize I am not really one to talk.

"The Grail was hidden away in Israel for many years, until the British knights came over during the crusades. They stole it and brought it back to England."

I drum my fingers on the table, impatient for Mag to get to the point. Honestly, I don't think I need to know the whole history of the world here.

"Fascinating. Really," I say, as the vampire pauses for breath. "Now can you just tell me how we can retrieve the thing already?"

He ignores me, of course, and drones on. He'd make a great history teacher. He's almost as boring as Ms. Dawson. "Somehow the ancient relic fell into the hands of the Lady of the Lake, Nimue, who lived on the island of Avalon. And that's where it's believed to be to this day. Buried far under the ground in a secret cave under the hill of Tor."

Now we're getting somewhere. "So is Avalon even a real place? Does it still exist? Can we get there and retrieve the Grail?" I know I'm asking questions faster than Magnus can answer them, but I'm way too desperate to help it.

"Yes, no, maybe," Magnus answers, matter-of-factly. "In that order."

"Um . . ."

"Yes, it was a real place," he clarifies. "But the priestesses of the past are long gone. It's not even technically an island anymore. Over the years the waters have turned to marshlands and the marshlands have since dried up. What used to be an island is now connected to the mainland of England."

"Gotcha."

"Present-day Avalon lies in a place called Glastonbury. A small, quiet village in the southwest of England."

"Do you think the Grail is still there somewhere?"

"Perhaps." Magnus strokes his chin thoughtfully. I love how he has just a tad of dangerous stubble lurking on his otherwise boyish face. I wonder if vampires have to shave. "I have heard rumors of an ancient druidic order that still makes its home in the village. They guard their secrets closely, but perhaps with the right persuasion, they may share their wisdom."

"So that's good, right?" I ask hopefully.

"I won't lie to you, Sunny. It's a definite long shot."

"Long shot, but not impossible shot." I'm determined to be Glass-Half-Full Chick here.

"Correct."

"So," I say, wanting to sum it all up. "All I have to do is fly to England, head to Glastonbury, find the members of an ancient hidden druidic order, and persuade them to take me to the Holy Grail, where I will be able to drink a drop of purifying blood and stop the transformation of me into a vampire."

"All before Saturday night at midnight," Magnus adds, looking at his watch.

I sigh. Things are looking not so half-full all of a sudden. I might have to change my name to Glass-Half-Empty Chick from now on. Actually, make that Glass-Drained-Dry Chick in this case.

First off, how the heck am I going to get to England? I can't exactly suggest an impromptu trip to my mom. She'd have all these ridiculous objections—her job, my school, no one to take care of our cat, Missy, etc., etc. Not to mention the fact that the old hippie has this outdated belief that airplanes are gas-guzzling monstrosities that wreak havoc on the environment and should not be flown except in emergencies like Grandma's funeral when there was no time to take her hybrid Toyota Prius.

Nope, the chances of me jetting off to jolly old England before Saturday at midnight are slim to none.

"Guess you can start calling me Vampire Sunny," I say with a desolate sigh. I take another mouthful of the blood wine. Might as well start developing a taste for the stuff.

"Hold on there," Magnus says. "You're not giving up that easily, are you?"

I look up from my glass. "I'm not living in a fantasy world, Mag. I'm not holding out false hope. There's absolutely no possible way I can swing by Glastonbury before Saturday night. I'm just being realistic."

Magnus picks up his own goblet and swirls the liquid around, staring at it for a moment. Then he looks at me. "I'll take you," he says, after a long pause.

I stare back at him, trying to ignore the sapphire blueness of his eyes. "What?" I ask, even though I heard him perfectly. It's simply that I can't believe what he said.

"To England. To Glastonbury. To Avalon. To find the Grail."

"You'd . . . you'd take me?" I repeat, knowing I'm not sounding like the most intelligent person at the moment. But still . . .

Magnus shrugs. "Sure. The coven has a few private jets. I can borrow one tomorrow night and we can head over." He sets down his glass. "I honestly don't know if we can find the Grail while we're there, but we can at least give it the old college try, right?"

I nod slowly, blown away by what he's just proposed. I mean, surely he has better things to do than to spend the week on a wild goose chase for the Holy Grail. And yet he's perfectly willing to set aside his plans to help me out.

"That's so . . . nice of you," I say, lamely.

He reaches over and takes my hand in his. Gah! His touch

sends chills down my arm, through my body, and down to my toes, like some kind of crazy electrical current. I resist the urge to squirm.

"Sunny," he says, tracing the back of my hand with a finger. Okay, he needs to stop doing that. Right now. "I hope you know I feel bloody awful about what I've put you through. If there's any way I can make it up to you, reverse the curse I've put you under, I want to do that."

I feel my insides melting, like a lime Popsicle in the sun. "Th-thank you," I murmur. "I really . . . appreciate that." I sound totally lame, but what else can I say?

He catches my eyes from across the table. I want to look away, but for some reason find myself totally mesmerized. He really does have amazing eyes. I wonder if he was born with them or if it's something you get as a perk from becoming a vamp. I supposed it would be a pretty good consolation prize. Lose your soul, gain captivating, irresistible eyes. Yeah, that would be cool, actually. Maybe you also get to lose weight and look like a supermodel. Blood would be pretty low in carbs, right? High in protein, rich in iron . . .

We're still staring at one another. This is getting a little weird. I should say something. Look away. Not start thinking about what I'll do if he reaches across the table, cups my chin in his hands, and kisses me senseless.

'Cause the scary thing is I think I might let him. In fact, I think I might kiss him back.

And that would be a very, very, very big mistake.

"Magnus!" cries a tortured-sounding voice. "There you are."

Magnus turns to address the voice, eliminating any kissing possibilities. Phew. What a relief. After all, I don't want to start any kind of relationship—physical or otherwise—with a creature of the night, especially not one like Mag. Though I do admit, he's a lot nicer and nobler than I first gave him credit. And he is rather good-looking . . .

I shake my head to get rid of my crazy thoughts and focus my attention on the guy who's approached our table.

"Jareth," Magnus greets our visitor, tight-lipped. Is he disappointed that our potential kissage was so rudely interrupted as well? Nah, I'm imagining things. "How are you this evening?"

"How am I?" Jareth asks with much incredulity. He's tall and good-looking in a Jude Law, British kind of way. Looks about eighteen, but is probably more like eight hundred. "How am I?" he repeats. He pulls up a chair and sits down. "The mighty leader of our coven has been tragically cut down and you ask me how I am?"

"We are all completely devastated by the loss of the master," Magnus agrees cautiously.

"Are you? Are all of you?" Jareth demands, scanning the room with eerie phosphorescent green eyes. See, I really am thinking the eye thing comes from the vampire curse. Who has such cool eyes in real life? (Well, besides that blind chick from season three of *America's Next Top Model*—not that I've ever watched that silly show. Really.) "For a people in mourning, you seem to be having a bloody good time."

He's got a point. No one here at Club Fang looks particularly broken up about the fact that their fearless leader was effectively dusted just twenty-four hours before. Sure, they're all wearing black, but I have a feeling that's more an everyday fashion statement than anything to do with paying their respects to Lucifent.

"We all grieve in our own ways, I am sure," Magnus replies evenly. "Some more openly than others."

"Bah! I would not let them show such disrespect myself," Jareth scoffs. "But I suppose you've got your own style of ruling. Speaking of, when do you plan to officially take command of the coven?"

What the . . . ? I whip my head around to stare at Magnus. What is this guy talking about? Taking command of the coven? Magnus?

Magnus shrugs. "I have some important business to attend to overseas," he explains. "When I return to the States, I will take my reign."

Holy crapola. Is he saying what I think he's saying? Magnus is taking over Lucifent's gig as king of the vampires? I had no idea the guy was that high up on the food chain. I figured he was just some everyday vampire type, but no! He's royalty. How cool is that?

Hmm, I wonder. Does this mean if I end up having to

remain a vampire forever that I get to be queen of the vampires? 'Cause that would be kind of cool. Especially if there's a tiara involved. I've always had a thing for tiaras . . .

"Do not stay away too long," Jareth advises sternly. His glowing emerald eyes really are a bit disconcerting. "There are others who would take advantage of your absence to legitimize their own rights to the throne."

"I am aware of their ambitions," Magnus says softly. "And I promise you, I do take them quite seriously."

"Very well, then," Jareth says, evidently satisfied by Mag's answer. "While you are gone, we will publicly throw our support behind you. It will not stop them, but perhaps it will delay their momentum."

"I thank you for that, brother." Magnus reaches over to pull the other vampire into an embrace. Midhug, he whispers something in his ear that for the life of me I can't make out. Not that I'm trying to eavesdrop on them or anything. I'm just curious. And hey, if I'm going to be stuck being queen, I figure I have the right to know all this stuff.

"You will make a fine coven leader," Jareth says, after parting from the hug. He rises from his seat and salutes Magnus. "I have much to do, so I bid you farewell. Good luck with your overseas adventure and I hope to confer with you on several matters when you get back."

"I shall look forward to it," Magnus says diplomatically, mirroring the vampire's salute and bowing his head.

Once Jareth's gone, I turn to Magnus, ready to get the 411 on the whole king thing.

"So what's the deal?" I ask eagerly. "You're like king of the vampires now? How come you didn't tell me? I mean, you'd think that might have come up in conversation."

Magnus shrugs. "I didn't think vampire politics would interest you."

"Vampire politics, no. My blood mate being king of the coven, hell yeah."

Magnus raises an eyebrow. "*Your* blood mate?"

I can feel my face heat into a major blush. Why did I just call him that? I didn't mean to. It just kind of slipped out.

"Um, yeah. Well, temporary blood mate, anyhow, right? Until we find the Grail and all."

"Ah." Magnus nods. If I didn't know better, I'd say he almost looks disappointed. Which is totally weird since I know that he doesn't want me as his blood mate any more than I want him to be mine. "Of course."

"So what's the deal?" I ask, going back to the subject at hand. "Are you king or what?"

"Technically, yes. I am next in line for the leadership position of our coven," Magnus says. "I was Lucifent's first fledgling, and therefore his most direct blood link. By vampire law, that makes me leader."

"Wow. How cool is that?" I cry. "King of the vampires. That's gotta be a good gig. You must be so psyched."

Magnus shakes his head. "Not especially, no," he says. "The position carries a lot of responsibilities and much danger. There are those, both in the outside world and right in our own coven, who seek to destroy the leader to further their own political agendas."

"Yeah, I heard Jareth say that. So there're going to be guys out to get you? Like vampire guys, not just the Slayer?" Hmm, maybe being king of the vampires ain't such a good gig after all.

"Yes. There will be 'guys out to get me,' as you so eloquently put it," Magnus says with a rueful smile. "But I am not concerned. With Jareth's men by my side I am well protected."

"Are they like bodyguards?"

"Soldiers. Jareth is leader of our royal army."

"Ah, I see." Wow. This vampire thing is super-organized. It's like this whole underground society, with kings and soldiers and evil guys up to no good . . .

Magnus rises from his seat. "We've dallied long enough. I must make preparations for our trip to England tomorrow."

"Okay," I agree, standing up and grabbing my purse off the floor. I glance at my watch. "I've got to get going anyhow or I'll miss curfew. Can't exactly jet off to England if I'm grounded."

We head out of Club Fang and into the night. I remember the first time we wandered through the parking lot just a few nights ago. At the time I had only thought about getting it on with a hot guy. Ha! If only I'd known what I was in for, I'd have gone shrieking into the night.

At least I think I would have.

"So if you're really going to have to take the throne and all and there are bad, power-hungry vamps that would love to usurp your power and become kings themselves, do you honestly have time to go traipsing off to England to help me find the Holy Grail?" I ask, turning to look at Mag. His already pale skin looks almost lustrous under the moonlight. I don't know how one vampire can be so delicious. It's so unfair.

"Don't get me wrong," I add. "I'm psyched to have your help, since there's no way I can do it on my own. It's just that, trying to be Unselfish Girl and all, it seems you've got a lot on your plate."

Magnus smiles—that gentle, reassuring smile he uses only occasionally, but each time it melts me a little. I can't believe I had thought he was an asshole when I first met him.

"You are my blood mate," he says simply, finding my hand and squeezing it with his own. "I would die for you."

Gah! A little warning before the touching would be nice. Mainly so I can resist the overwhelming urge to morph into a jiggly pile of Jell-O, thank you very much.

"You'd . . . die . . . for me?" I manage to choke out. I've got to lighten the mood here. "Technically aren't you already dead?"

He chuckles at that and pulls on my hand so I end up facing him. We're way too close now. Way overstepping the three-foot-bubble rule. I can feel his breath on my face. His hands moving to my waist. I draw in a raspy breath, trying to sustain some semblance of control.

"Um," I say, suddenly not at my most articulate. My heart is beating out of control and I feel like I'm going to keel over. How can one guy have so much sex appeal?

Then I remember. The Vampire Scent. I'm not really attracted to him whatsoever. It's just those pheromones of his that have got my juices flowing. Ha!

I pull back. "Is there a way you can turn off the Vampire Scent thing?" I ask. "'Cause it's kind of throwing me off my game here."

He laughs and yanks me closer, our bodies now flush against one another, my curves molding into his hard, flat planes of stomach muscle. He feels so good I can barely stand up.

"As my blood mate, you are immune to my Vampire Scent," he whispers in my ear, tickling the lobe with his breath. "Any attraction you feel is all your own."

See? I truly *am* doomed.

"Eh, please. You've totally got it wrong. I don't, er, feel any attraction," I manage to say, reluctantly pulling myself away from his embrace. "I mean . . . um . . ."

He releases me with a grin. "Right. No attraction whatsoever. Good to know." He doesn't look like he believes me for one second. Which is understandable, since I don't even believe myself.

"I've, um, got to get going," I say, stepping backward a few steps. In fact, I need to ditch this scene ASAP—before

I throw myself at him and succumb to the passions of the night. (Wow, do I sound like a romance novel or what?) "Don't want to piss off my mom and get grounded for missing curfew for the third night in a row."

Magnus nods. "Of course. I understand." I strain to see if he looks disappointed, but he's keeping a complete poker face. "It is probably for the best. I have much to do."

"Great. Okay." So why do I feel this deep sense of disappointment all of a sudden? What did I want him to do, grab me and drag me back to his lair and have his wicked way with me against my will? He's a gentleman. A retired knight in shining armor, trained in the code of chivalry. Not some barbarian caveman with no respect for women.

"So when do we leave for England?" I ask, turning to walk toward my parked car. Magnus follows, a few steps behind.

"As soon as possible," he says. "I shall arrange for the private jet tonight. Meet me at the Manchester Airport tomorrow at four P.M. and we will go from there."

"Okay," I say, fishing through my purse for my keys. I unlock and pull open the front door. "Then, till tomorrow, I guess."

"Till tomorrow," Magnus repeats.

We both stand there for a moment, as if each is unwilling to be the first to walk away. Why does this have to be so awkward?

Finally Magnus turns to leave.

"Mag?" I call after him.

He stops and turns back to look at me. "Yes?" he asks in a low rumbly voice that totally turns me on all over again.

"Thank you."

He nods slowly and starts walking again. I hear him mumbling something under his breath. Something I can't quite make out. But something that sounds an awful lot like "Anything for you, my love."

But I'm sure I'm just hearing things, right?

15

But I'm a Vampire,
Not a Druggie!

I arrive home only three minutes after curfew. I probably broke every speed limit in the book to make it, but I figured if any cops were going to start writing tickets, I'd stick them with my Vampire Scent. It has to be said, that sure is one useful supernatural power. (Except of course when it turns on lesbian secretaries and weirdo perv teachers. That I could do without.)

I unlock the front door to my house and step inside. The place is completely dark. I wonder if everyone's already in bed. Though I suppose Rayne's probably still awake, typing away on her computer as usual. Which is good 'cause I've got to work out a plan with her. Since I can't exactly tell Mom I'm skipping town for a couple days to make an impromptu trip to England hoping to find the lost cup of Christ that will purify my blood and remove the vampire taint, my dear sister is going to have to cover for me.

I enter the hallway, trying to tiptoe. No need to wake everyone up. But my Keep Quiet plan is immediately foiled when I accidentally step on a loose, creaky flagstone. Damn.

A light switches on in the kitchen, making me jump back in surprise, my heart leaping to my throat.

"Sunny? Is that you?"

I breathe a sigh of relief. Just Mom. For a split second I was thinking the Slayer might have figured out where I lived and was having a midnight snack while waiting to dust me.

Then again, it's very possible that a curfew convo with mom could be more painful.

"Yeah, mom. It's me." I glance longingly at the stairs that lead up to my dark, cozy bedroom. The fluorescent kitchen light is giving me a headache, even from here. But I know there's no way I'm going to escape a lecture at this point.

"Do you want some Tofutti?" she asks. "I'm making myself a dish."

"No thanks," I say, reluctantly heading into the kitchen. Only my mom would consider ice cream made out of tofu a special treat. I prefer Ben & Jerry's Chunky Monkey myself, and hey, don't those guys work to save the planet, too?

I plop down at the breakfast bar and rub my eyes with my fists. I'm so tired. I haven't had a good night's sleep since this whole thing started. At the same time, I feel really wired and

I doubt I'll be able to get any sleep tonight either. At least until dawn, and then Rayne will have to drag me out of bed. I wonder if I can fake sick and avoid school . . . I really need a good day's sleep.

"Are you sure you don't want any? I have some sugar-free carob syrup to put over it," Mom says, holding up the jar. I cringe. I didn't like that imitation hippie chocolate stuff before I became a vampire. I'm certainly not going to develop a taste now.

My mom finishes squirting carob on her Tofutti and puts the bottle and container back in the fridge and freezer, respectively. Then she sits across from me at the breakfast bar and spoons a large scoop into her mouth.

"Mmm," she says, licking her lips. "You don't know what you're missing."

I laugh. "Oh yes, I do. Remember, you forced us to eat this stuff as kids. I didn't taste real ice cream till fourth grade."

"Yes, and that was only because Evil Aunt Edna corrupted you. One mouthful and you became a hopeless junk food junkie," Mom says with a sigh, taking another spoonful. "And you never looked back."

I smile. I know she's not really upset. She raised Rayne and me to be our own people. To have our own thoughts and dreams and ideas. And diets. She taught us her way, but never insisted we follow it. She's cool like that.

"So how did your test go today?" Mom asks, studying me

with eyes that on the surface look completely innocent. But I know she's asking a weighted question.

"Um, fine. Fine," I mumble. I really suck at lying. Unlike Rayne, who could enter the Lying Olympics and win the gold medal, hands down. I mean, I thought twins were supposed to have identical DNA, but somehow Rayne got the Good Liar gene and I got stuck with the Face Gives Everything Away one.

"Mmm-hmm," my mom says, sounding more than a bit skeptical. "And your night tonight? Did you have a good night?"

"Yeah, it was okay," I say, praying for no follow-ups. But it seems the interrogation gods have no plans to show me mercy.

"Where did you go?"

"Um, a coffeehouse in Nashua." Figure I might as well be as truthful as possible, without mentioning the whole vampire thing, of course.

"I see." My mom presses her lips together for a moment. "And what did you do there?"

"Drank coffee . . . ?" Well, duh.

"And who did you drink this coffee with?"

I squirm in my seat. "Er, a few friends."

Please don't ask who, please don't ask who, please don't ask who.

"Who?"

Damn.

"Um, there was Rachel and Charity . . ." *Who gave me a*

goblet of their own blood to drink before taking off, I imagine telling her. *Wasn't that just so nice of them? And then Jareth showed up. Vampire General, you know. Out to protect Magnus, king of the vampires and my blood mate for eternity, unless I can swing by England tomorrow to pick up the Holy Grail. You don't mind if I skip school for that, do you?*

I wonder how many milliseconds it would take for her to dial the men in white coats?

"Rachel and Charity?" Mom repeats, tapping her temple with her index finger. "Don't think I've heard you mention them before. Do they go to school with you?"

"Man, what is it with the third degree, Mom?" I retort, unable to hold back my guilty annoyance a moment longer. "I mean, since when do you care who I hang out with or what I'm doing?"

Jeez. I take back all that cool mom stuff. Every single last coolness point awarded over the years. Gone. Tonight, she's as much a pain in the butt as the rest of my friends' moms.

"Since when do I care?" she repeats, raising her eyebrows. Uh-oh. I so don't like the raised eyebrows thing. It never turns out good. "You want to know since when? I guess it'd be since your sister told me you were studying at the library all night. Alone."

Oh.

Damn it, I knew I should have called Rayne on her cell on the way home to find out if she'd taken it upon herself to cover for me.

"Oh. Right," I say. I've got to save this or I'll be grounded and it's going to be a heck of a lot more difficult to get to England with Magnus. "We were studying. Drinking coffee and studying. This is sort of a library-slash-coffeehouse kind of place, really. It's the new 'in' thing, actually. Everyone says coffeehouses are the new libraries. Like you get your caffeine and then you study. It's great and—"

"Sunny, are you on drugs?" Mom suddenly asks, point-blank.

I stop talking immediately, but I think my mouth is still hanging open in shock.

"Am I on . . . drugs?" I repeat incredulously. She's got to be kidding me, right?

"It's a simple question."

She's not kidding. I can tell by the oh-so-serious expression on her face. I can't believe it!

"I know it's a simple question, but why would you ask it?" I demand, very insulted at this point. "Do I *seem* like I'm on drugs?"

My mom shrugs. "Actually, yes, you do. You're out till all hours of the night and you lie about where you are. You throw up first thing in the morning. Your eyes are completely bloodshot and your pupils dilated. Your hands are trembling and you're paler than Rayne with her pancake makeup on. So, yes, I have to say, you do seem like you're on drugs."

Okay, fine. She's got a point. But still . . .

"I'm not, though," I deny, knowing I sound totally lame.

But how can I defend myself without spilling the crazy truth, which she'll never believe anyway?

"Sunny, you can tell me if you are," Mom says, putting down her Tofutti spoon. "I know that many teens experiment. I myself dabbled plenty back in the seventies. Pot, acid, you name it, I probably tried it. But if you're going to partake, you need to do it safely. And I want to make sure you're not doing anything dangerous. I love you and I don't want to lose you."

I seriously want to bang my head against the table in frustration. I can't believe my mom thinks I'm doing drugs. And I have no idea how I'm going to convince her otherwise. I mean, everything she's listed is basically a symptom of me turning into a vampire, yet I can't very well tell her that.

"I can assure you, Mom," I say, swallowing back my annoyance. I know she's just trying to help, but I'm tired and cranky and just want to go to bed. "I am not, nor am I planning to be anytime in the near or far future, on any kind of drugs."

My mom sighs deeply, running a hand through her long graying hair. She always jokes that Rayne is the cause of all her premature grays. Tonight, I think she's putting the blame on me as well.

"You know, I had hoped we'd have the kind of mother-daughter relationship where you'd feel free to talk to me about this kind of stuff," she says sadly. "I know it sounds cliché, but I wanted to be your friend as well as your mother.

Someone you'd share things with and know that I wouldn't judge you for them. I wanted to have a different kind of relationship with you and Rayne than I had with my own mother."

"You do. We are friends," I cry, reaching over to place my hand over her forearm, succumbing to a major guilt attack. "I do tell you everything. I love you, Mom. It's just honestly, this time there's nothing to tell. I'm simply not on drugs. Period. End of story."

My mother nods slowly. I can see a tear slip from the corner of her eye. Great. Now I've totally upset her. But what can I do? I can't tell her the truth this time. There's no way. But by keeping silent, I'm making it seem like I don't trust her.

Gah, this is so hard.

"Sunny, I hate to do this to you," Mom says, swiping her wayward tear on her sleeve. "But I feel it's for your own good."

Uh-oh.

"If you're not on drugs, then you're obviously sick or something. 'Cause you don't look good. So I need you to stay in until you start looking better."

"You're grounding me?" Crap. I can't be grounded. I have to sneak off to England tomorrow. How can I sneak off to England tomorrow if I'm grounded?

"No, not grounding, exactly."

"But I can't go out."

"Right."

"At all."

"You can go to school . . ."

"So how is that not grounding?" I demand.

She shrugs. "I guess it is. I just always hated that term. It sounds so . . . totalitarian."

"Then why be a fascist dictator?" I try.

"Sunny, please." My mother rubs her temples with her forefingers. "It's late. I'm tired. You have school tomorrow. Go to bed."

"Fine. Whatever," I retort. I jump off the bar stool I was sitting on and head toward the hall. "Some cool mom you turned out to be," I mutter under my breath, secretly hoping she can hear me.

16

The Great Twin Caper

I trudge up the stairs, totally bummed out, and hang a left toward Rayne's bedroom, praying she'll still be awake. If anyone will know what to do in a sitch like this, she will. After all, she's the original bad girl in the McDonald household. I'm just playing catch-up.

I see a crack of light under her door and lightly knock. "Rayne? Are you awake?" I whisper.

"Yeah, of course. Come in."

I push open the door and enter the room. She's got it dimly lit with a black light, and cutouts of bats and spiders on cottony webs glow green on her walls.

She's sitting at her computer, with some kind of role-playing computer game up on her screen. She signs off as I enter and invites me to sit on the bed with her.

"So how'd it go?" she asks eagerly. "Did Mag come up with a way to turn you back?"

"Yeah, sort of. He researched and says he's found something that will purify my blood and remove all the vampire taint for good."

"Great!"

"No, not great, actually. I mean, great that he found something, but not so great that the something in question isn't exactly sold at Wal-Mart."

"Great stuff never is." Rayne shakes her head. "So what is it? Eye of newt? Mummy dust? Vial of slime from the Bog of Eternal Stench?"

"Worse. Blood from the Holy Grail."

"Ouch." Rayne pulls her feet up on the bed so she's sitting cross-legged. "How the heck are you going to get hold of that? Does the Grail even exist?"

So I relate all that Magnus told me about the Grail, its supposed resting place in Avalon, and our impending trip. She looks impressed.

"First a tour of the vampire coven, now a holiday in jolly old England. You're so lucky," she says when I'm finished. "I'm totally jealous."

"Please. I'd so rather have you go in my place," I say with a sigh. "I have no idea how I'm even going to get there."

"I thought you said Mag had a private plane. That's amazingly cool that he has a private plane. I bet it's all luxurious with beds and everything. You know, if I had the opportunity to be with Magnus on a private plane with beds on it, I'd be an official mile-high club member before we landed. Maybe even before we took off." She grins evilly as I swat her on the knee.

"Yeah, yeah," I say, rolling my eyes. It never ceases to amaze me that whatever the subject matter at hand, Rayne can think of a way to relate it to sex.

"What? You don't think I could do it?"

I laugh. "Are you kidding? I'm just shocked to learn you've never done it before. I figured you'd be a mile-high platinum member in good standing, Slut Girl." Now it's Rayne's turn to swat me. "Hey! You hit way too hard!" I protest, rubbing my abused knee.

"You know, for a vampire, you're a real wimp, Sun," Rayne says with a laugh as she collapses on the bed, staring up at the ceiling. Like mine, hers is also lit up by glow-in-the-dark stars affixed during our misspent youths. "So when are you going to England?"

"Well, I'm supposed to leave tomorrow night. But I don't know how I'm going to get out of the house. Mom's evidently decided that I'm some crackhead and has subsequently put me under house arrest."

"Are you kidding me? Mom's grounded you? Wow. She

must be really worried." Rayne sits up. "After all, she's not ex-actly the grounding type."

"I know, I know," I groan. "But she thinks I'm all on drugs or something. 'Cause of how I look and stuff."

"Puh-leeze. You on drugs? Come on!" Rayne snorts in disgust. "She knows you better than that. I mean, I can see her saying *I'm* on drugs. But you? Give me a break."

I shrug, for once not arguing with her over her Sunny the Innocent spiel. I just wish Mom shared her opinion. It'd make things a lot easier.

"So now I'm royally screwed," I say. "I don't want to in-cur the wrath of the Momster, but my life as I know it depends on this trip to England. I have no idea what I'm gonna do."

"Hmm." Rayne taps her finger on her knee in thought. "Well, why don't I be you?" she suggests at last.

"Huh?" I scrunch up my eyes in confusion. "You mean like you go to England with Magnus?"

"Please. I wish. But no," Rayne says, shaking her head. "What I mean is I can pretend to be the grounded you. And you can pretend to be the me that wants to go sleep over her friend Spider's house. Then you can really sneak off to England."

"You have a friend named Spider?" I ask, raising an eye-brow. "Is that a male friend or female one?"

"Um, well, a little of each, actually. Long story. But Sun, you're missing the point here."

I try to shake the image of the androgynous "Spider" and

focus. "So," I recap, "you'd be willing to sit home and play grounded me while I jet off to England to find the Holy Grail?"

Rayne shrugs. "It's a sucky gig, I know. But I sorta feel responsible for getting you into this mess. So sure. I'll be the grounded you."

"Don't you think Mom might catch on? I mean, it'd be ten thousand gazillion times worse if she figured it out. And then you'd get in trouble, too."

"Hello? Earth to Sunny!" Rayne says, waving a hand in front of my face. "In case you don't remember, we are so identical that a superpowerful creature of the night couldn't even tell us apart. You think nearsighted, hippy-dippy Mom will have the slightest clue?"

I think about it for a moment. "You have a point."

"Of course I do," Rayne says, bobbing her head in enthusiasm. "It's perfect. I'll just act real boring and goody two-shoes and she'll never know the diff."

I have to bite my lip not to respond, reminding myself that she's totally saving my life here and I need to cut her a little slack in the tact department.

"Okay, then. It's settled," I say. "Tomorrow morning, you tell Mom you're staying with Spider and then once we're in school we'll switch clothes."

"Sounds like a plan," Rayne says, eyes shining. She loves stuff like this. She pauses for a minute, then adds, "Though I have to say I so wish *I* were going to be the one traveling to England with Magnus."

I look over at her, surprised. "You don't still have a thing for him, do you?" I ask cautiously, trying to sound casual.

Oh, please don't say you have a thing for him, I mentally beg. *That would so not be good.*

My mind wanders back to our night. Magnus stroking the back of my hand. My body pressed against his. Our almost-kiss. I wonder what Rayne would say if she knew about my extracurricular Magnus activities. Would she be mad? If she's still crushing on him, then I have a pretty good idea that she would be. And I don't want to incur the wrath of Rayne.

My twin sighs, long and hard, and throws herself dramatically onto the bed. "Of course I do," she moans. "He's meant to be my perfect match. I mean, I don't know if he told you, but they don't just randomly hook up vamps and humans as blood mates. There are scientific studies and everything. It's very complicated. And after all that, the Council decided that Magnus and I should be destined to spend eternity with one another. And now, because of a stupid, stupid mistake, he's stuck with someone who doesn't even want him."

"I—" I start to protest, then bite down on my lower lip. *Definitely don't want to go there, Sun.* "How do they determine blood mate compatibility?" I ask instead, trying to sound completely detached.

"DNA. Your DNA is compared to the vampire's to determine compatibility," Rayne explains. "You'd know this if you read my blog."

"Yeah, yeah, read the blog, I know, I know," I mutter. But inside I'm thinking something completely different.

Because one thing you may or may not know about identical twins is that they also have identical DNA. Which means technically, if Magnus and Rayne are perfect blood mates . . .

So are Magnus and I.

17

Swapping Spit with the Sex God

Amazingly enough, the next morning, things start off going exactly to plan. Rayne tells Mom about her sleepover at Spider's and Mom makes offhanded comments like "Okay" and "Have fun." She doesn't even ask who or what a "Spider" is, thank goodness.

Nope, she's way more interested in reminding me that I'm still very grounded. (Though she uses the phrase "resting at home until you feel better" instead of the G-word—something she must have read in the *Hip Mama Handbook*.) But whatever the terminology, the bottom line is the same: I'm to come home directly after school. I am not to pass Go. I am not to collect $200. (After all, I might use it to finance a big crack rock for breakfast, right?)

I try to act all agreeable and normal and non-druggie-like, which turns out to be more difficult than I anticipated, mainly due to my exhausted, bloodshot eyes refusing to open all the way in our bright, sunshiny kitchen. Bleh.

Luckily this morning there's carrot and buckwheat pan-cakes sans garlic on the menu and I manage to wolf them down without puking. They do nothing, however, to stop the ravenous thirst for blood that's been raging inside me since I first opened my eyes. You know how when you've got your period you crave chocolate like crazy? I've got that kind of craving for blood this morning, but times about a million.

I want blood. I need blood. I'd do almost anything to get it. Gross, I know, but what can I say? Hi, my name is Sunny and I'm a bloodoholic.

At one particularly low point, I find myself mesmerized by a particular vein in my mother's neck. Imagine, here's me, watching it, fantasizing about the delicious, syrupy blood flowing freely inside it. The vein pulses, almost as if it has a life of its own, and I envision sinking my teeth into it and just sucking away like mad.

Then Mom catches me staring.

"What?" she asks, touching her neck self-consciously.

"Nothing, sorry," I say, dragging my eyes away from the tempting little pulse. I can't believe I've just been caught eye-ing up my mother like she's a piece of prime rib.

I need serious help.

To prevent further embarrassment, I excuse myself and

head to the bathroom, locking the door behind me. I peer into the mirror. Wow. If I were my mom I'd think I was on drugs too. I look like crap. My face is even paler now—like Michael Jackson pale—and my lips are just as blood red. If I end up remaining a vampire for eternity, I'll never have to re-stock on lipstick.

My eyes are dark and bloodshot and my pupils are totally dilated. I try squirting a little Visine in them, hoping it will do the trick, but I'm not sure it makes much difference.

And then there's my teeth. But I don't even want to get into that. It'd just freak you out.

At school I'm a walking zombie. Seriously, if I don't get this vampire thing straightened out soon, I'm going to end up flunking out. There's no way I can concentrate on what the teachers are saying in my current state. And I'm utterly un-able to focus my eyes under the fluorescent lights, meaning I can barely read the pop quiz questions from English class.

When the final bell rings, I'm thankful to head to the girls' locker room, where I'm supposed to meet Rayne to change clothes and start The Great Identical Twin Switcheroo.

Unfortunately, before I can make it to the girls' only haven, I'm stopped by a boy.

Not just any boy, however. I'm stopped by Jake. Jake Wilder, to be exact.

My heart flutters a little as he steps in front of me, his dark, brooding eyes raking over my body like I'm some gour-met dessert and he hasn't eaten in a week.

He wants me. Badly. His desire radiates from him.

I shiver.

"Sunny," he cries, his normally deep, velvet voice sounding a little hoarser than usual. "Where have you been?"

I cock my head in confusion. What is he talking about? I've been at school. Like always. "Um, hi, Jake," I say, a little warily. "What do you mean, where have I been?" I steal a glance at my watch. Magnus's plane leaves in one hour and I've got to change clothes first. But I can't exactly blow off the Sex God, now can I? After all, what if he has some important prom thing he needs to ask me about? Like what color my dress is so he can get a matching cummerbund, or something.

Crap. That reminds me—I don't have a dress yet! Haven't exactly had any time to shop for one. You know, this vampire stuff is really wreaking havoc on my everyday schedule.

"I've been looking everywhere for you. It's weird, but . . ." Jake runs a hand through his already seemingly tousled hair. Honestly, he looks a little ill. But then again, I look like death warmed over, so I'm really not one to talk. "I can't stop thinking about you. Even when I'm sleeping . . ." He pauses, red-faced. "I have these dreams where you—"

"Okay, Jake," I interrupt, putting a hand over his mouth. "We're headed deep into TMI territory here." Even though secretly I would love to hear about Jake Wilder's erotic dreams, especially if they involve me, I think I might regret it in the long run . . .

Suddenly, without any kind of warning, Jake grabs me by the waist and pulls me close to him, covering my surprised mouth with a deep kiss. For a moment I can't breathe. At first I think this is because I'm so turned on by the fact that I'm being kissed by a Sex God. Then I realize Jake's crushing my rib cage.

"Mmhmm," I protest.

Jake loosens his hold and his desperate, breathless kisses travel from my lips down my neck. I do my best to scan the gymnasium, hoping no one's around to see us—I'm so not into PDA. Still, for Jake Wilder, I should probably make an exception.

As he nibbles on my neck, his hands rove up and down my back, almost clawing at me, as if he can't get enough. I am so blown away that he's doing this, I've been rendered speechless. I can't believe Jake Wilder is groping me in the middle of our high school gym. If you had told me I'd be accosted by Jake Wilder in our gym a week before, I would have laughed and laughed and said things like, "Yeah, right" and "Good one!"

Then again, I probably wouldn't have bought the whole vampire thing either. I've got a much more open mind now.

"You smell so good," Jake whispers, his traveling lips now touring my ear. "You're so beautiful."

"Um, thanks?" I say, not quite sure what to do or how to react. I sneak another glance at my watch, then scold myself for doing so.

What am I doing? Who cares if I'm a few minutes late? Magnus is a thousand-year-old vampire. He has eternal life. So technically speaking, he's got all the time in the world. And who knows how much longer I'll be able to make out with Jake Wilder? I mean, once I turn into a human again, I assume he'll go back to not acknowledging my existence. I've got to take advantage of his intoxication.

Then again, that's kind of sick, isn't it? I mean, how can I enjoy a make-out session with someone who's not really into me—who just *thinks* he is? Suddenly, the kisses aren't sexy. Just kind of gross. And sloppy too, now that I'm being honest. I mean, who really, at the end of the day, enjoys a slimy tongue jammed into her ear? Even if it is a tongue belonging to the resident school Sex God.

I gently push Jake away. "I'm sorry," I say. "But I have to go."

"Please don't go!" he begs, his deep, soulful eyes boring into my skull. Yikes. How hard is this? The man I've loved from afar for two years now is begging me to stay like some kind of lovesick puppy. "Sunny, I want you," he says, reaching over to brush a lock of hair out of my face.

I take a step back, using every last ounce of willpower. "You don't," I say firmly. "You think you do, but you really don't."

Jake's face crumples with a look of devastation. "How can you say that?" he asks.

"Sorry Jake, gotta go." I pat him on the shoulder. "Things to do, people to see, you know how it is. I'll catch you around though."

Crushed Sex God nods desolately. "We're still going to the prom, though, right?" he asks.

"Of course," I say in my most reassuring voice. *If once I reverse the vampire thing you still want to go with me*, I add silently as I say my good-byes and head into the locker room.

And that seems to me a big fat "if."

18

Leaving—on a Vamp Plane

Rayne is waiting for me in the locker room.

"What happened?" she asks. "You look all bedraggled-like."

"Jake Wilder happened."

Rayne raises an eyebrow. "Ooh, Jake Wilder. Is that a good thing, then?"

"Sort of. I guess. Well, not really." I lean against the nearest locker and sigh deeply. I'm so confused. "It was weird, actually. I mean, don't get me wrong—I have no moral issue with Jake sticking his tongue down my throat, believe me. But still, the whole time he was doing it, I couldn't help but think how he doesn't *really* like me. How he's just bewitched by the Vampire Scent thing and has no idea what he's doing.

And suddenly, the impromptu make-out session didn't seem so exciting."

My twin nods in sympathy. "Sorry, Sun," she says. "I can see how that would suck. But hopefully you'll be back to normal before you know it and then you can see once and for all if Jake likes you as a person. Who knows," she adds, "maybe the vampire thing is just a coincidence and he's really been pining for you from afar for years and has finally worked up the courage to talk to you."

"Right. And maybe someday you'll end up being an investment banker with a minivan, a husband who wears paisley ties, and three Gap kids."

Rayne snorts. "Touché."

"It doesn't matter anyhow," I say, pushing myself off the locker. "I've got to concentrate on my mission. Jake and his weird new obsession must wait. Turning back into a human takes precedence."

I slip out of my jeans and tank top and hand them to Rayne. She in turn offers up a long black skirt and peasant blouse that reek of patchouli.

"Make sure you wipe all the goop off your face," I remind her as she slips into my jeans, complaining how awful they make her thighs look. "Mom's never going to buy the idea of me channeling *Gossip Girl*'s Little J."

"I know, I know," Rayne says. "Relax, will you? It's going to be fine. We're not going to get caught. You'll get to England no problem, find the Grail, turn back into a human, and live happily ever after with dopey, puppy-dog Jake Wilder."

"One can only dream," I answer with a dash of dramatic flair. I pull the peasant blouse and skirt on and glance at myself in the mirror. This is not a good look for me. And Magnus, safe and sound in some very now-looking Armani ensemble, is going to have a field day.

Not that I care what he thinks, obviously.

After the clothes swapping and face washing, Rayne drives me to the airport where I'm to meet Magnus. I'm not very talkative on the way there, mainly 'cause I'm still very nervous about this whole thing. I mean, think about it for a second. I'm now leaving the country with a man I barely know, who incidentally happens to be an immortal creature of the night.

Not exactly your typical 7-Eleven Cherry Slurpee run.

All too soon, Rayne pulls up to the private hangar where Magnus says the coven keeps its jet. I had this strange idea in my head that Air Vampire would be a black plane with a blood-red interior. But I guess that would be too obvious, 'cause the real-life vehicle in question just looks like your typical, nondescript private plane.

I hug Rayne good-bye before exiting the car.

"Good luck," she whispers. "Take good care of Magnus for me."

"I will," I say, getting that lovely guilty feeling back in the

pit of my stomach. Maybe it's just my thirst for blood. I hope
Magnus has a good supply on board, 'cause I feel like I'm going to pass out from hunger.

I get out of the car and head for the plane. A man in a pilot's uniform greets me with a friendly smile.

"Hello," he says in a clipped British accent. "You must be
Ms. McDonald."

"Yup, that's me," I reply. "But you can call me Sunny."

He gestures to the stairs leading up to the plane. "You
may board at your convenience, ma'am."

I glance around the tarmac. "Where's Magnus?"

"Inside," the pilot informs me. "He is taking a nap at the
moment."

Ah, that makes sense. I thought it seemed too early—too
daylight—for him to be up and about. He must have holed
himself up in the plane before dawn and made plans to wake
up midflight, once the sun's retreated from the horizon.

I head up the stairs, turning to give one last wave to
Rayne. The nervous feeling starts nagging at my stomach
once again. But I squash it and attempt to step confidently
into the plane.

I forget my nerves completely when my eyes fall on the
jumbo jet's interior décor. Just like the coven, this place reeks
of luxury. Decked out in gold and velvet, it's a display of
wealth that's almost obscene. There are soft leather arm-
chairs and ridiculously huge plasma TVs. Bottles of red wine

(blood?) chilling in silver buckets and state-of-the-art laptops sitting on etched-glass desks. This is truly the Ritz of the airplane world.

"Please have a seat and fasten your seat belt," the pilot says, coming up behind me. "We'll be taking off shortly."

I comply, still blown away by all the extravagance. Being a vampire sure has some perks. Then again, Mag is the next in line to be king. I wonder if the plane is available to all the vamps or just the ones in high places.

I switch on the television, delighted to find it has every movie under the sun. I pick a light comedy, eager to be distracted, and settle into my über-comfy seat. A minute later, I'm out like a light.

"Sunny?"

I open one eye, then the other, slightly annoyed at being disturbed from my slumber. Magnus is peering over me, a slight smile playing at the corner of his mouth.

"Are you going to sleep all night?" he asks, poking me lightly in the shoulder.

"Grumph," I reply, trying to roll to my other side to ignore him. Unfortunately, like a good girl, I'd fastened my seat belt so I have limited maneuverability.

"Wake up. We're here," he instructs.

"Here?"

"In England. The town of Bristol, to be exact."

"What time is it?"

He glances at his watch. Rolex, of course. "It's just before three A.M. local time. We've got to get to our safe house before the sun rises."

I yawn, stretching my hands above my head. "Safe house?" I ask. I can't believe we're in England. That I slept through the whole flight. I didn't even get a chance to enjoy all the luxuries the plane had to offer. Darn. Maybe on the way back . . .

Magnus nods. "You know I can't get caught out in the sunlight. I've arranged with a local vamp coven for us to stay with them until nightfall. Then we'll travel by car to Glastonbury. It's about an hour trip."

"Oh. Okay," I say. I had forgotten about Magnus's aversion to the sun. This meant our trip was going to have to take longer than I anticipated. I had stupidly assumed we'd get to England, grab the Grail, and head straight back to America, arriving just after school ended. Hopefully Rayne will be able to keep up the twin charade a bit longer.

I unfasten my seat belt and follow Magnus out of the plane. There's a limo (of course!) waiting and a properly dressed chauffeur opens the door for us to climb inside.

Once settled and on our way, Magnus turns to me. "So how are you holding up?" he asks, to his credit sounding genuinely concerned.

"Fine."

"No. I mean, really," he insists. "It's okay. You can tell me. I'm sure it's been a bloody terrible experience for you. It's hard enough for those who have been properly trained. But to go through all this completely unprepared . . . Well, I can only imagine how hard it must be."

I nod slowly. "It's really strange," I admit. "My mom thinks I'm on drugs. I've got all these weird cravings. I feel sick to my stomach all the time. It's hard to see under fluorescent lights and the sun beats down on my skin as if it could blister it at any moment. And," I add, reluctantly, "I feel like I'm dying of thirst."

There. I said it. I admitted I wanted—make that needed—blood. I'm officially a freak of nature. But then again, so's he.

Magnus nods sympathetically. "I'm sure you're ravenous by this point. I had some wine for you on the plane, but I didn't want to wake you. Figured you needed all the sleep you could get." He pats me lightly on the knee. "Hang in there. When we get to the coven, we will be able to feed."

Oh goody. I can't wait.

19

The Coven—England Style

Ten minutes later, we pull up to an old English manor. An ancient scary-looking one like you always see in the movies, with wrought-iron gates and scads of unhappy ghosts going around and haunting everyone. But Magnus assures me the vampires who live here keep the place clean of any sort of poltergeists.

The interior of the mansion is less ostentatious than the American coven. It's also not underground, which means all the windows have had to be boarded up to make sure no sunshine slips in. An old vampire (I mean, they're all old, technically speaking, but this one actually has the liver-spotted hands to prove it) greets us, bowing low to Magnus.

"Well met, good sir. I hear you will be taking over The

Blood Coven," he says in a low, respectful voice. His accent reminds me of the ones you hear vampires use in the movies. Like from Transylvania or something.

Magnus returns the bow. "Indeed. But first I must attend to some important business in Glastonbury. So I do thank you for allowing us weary travelers a place to rest."

It's so interesting to me how formal vamps are when they chat with one another. It's like there's some secret vampire-speak they've all mastered. Then again, I guess in the era when they were growing up human, that's how people really talked. They probably prefer it and only learn slang to keep up appearances among mortals.

"Of course. It is an honor to host you and your blood mate," the grandpa vampire says. The tux he's wearing totally screams Dracula wanna-be, but I'm not opening my big mouth this time. I mean, really. For all I know, the guy *is* Dracula.

Drac escorts us down the hallway and up a large winding flight of stairs. The place looks very badly kept up, to tell you the truth. There's cobwebs everywhere. If I end up stuck as a vamp forever, I'm living in the luxury New England coven instead. Way more my style.

The doors to the bedrooms look like vaults in a bank, each with its own keypad lock. Drac picks a door, seemingly at random, and enters a code. The door swings silently open into a blackened room.

Magnus bows low again. "Thank you, my good sir," he says.

Drac returns his bow and then retreats down the hall. Magnus ushers me into the room.

Where there is only one bed.

"Um." I scan the room. "Hmm."

"What's wrong?" Magnus asks, shutting the door behind us. He's standing directly behind me, and I can feel his breath on my neck, which is a tad disconcerting. I step into the room to add space between us.

"Doesn't Drac have a second bedroom? I mean, this is a mansion, right?"

"Drac?" Magnus repeats, raising an eyebrow in question.

I blush. Forgot that was just my nickname for the guy. "You know, our illustrious host."

Magnus grins. "He does look a bit like the legendary Dracula, doesn't he?" he admits. "We all used to tease him about that in our younger days . . ."

"Um, can we walk down memory lane later, Mag? Right now we need to concentrate on the big picture," I interrupt. I don't mean to be rude, but there's a pressing issue to be dealt with here. "We have one room. One bed. And two of us."

Magnus nods. "Indeed. I am sure our host has assumed that we would share a bed, as we are blood mates, after all."

"Well, we all know what assuming does, right? Makes an *ass* out of *you* and *me*."

"I'm sorry, Sunny. But if I were to ask him for a second room, it would raise far too many questions. Questions that might undermine my newfound position as coven leader."

"Ah," I say, realizing what he's saying. "So if you were to say you screwed up and did an unauthorized bite on some poor innocent girl like me, then people might say you're unfit to be king?"

He nods. "Indeed. And while I do not relish the idea of taking over the coven, it would be better that I do so than to let those seize control who do not have the coven's best interests at heart."

"Gotcha," I say. "So we have to play loving blood mates in front of the other vamps."

"Basically, yes."

"And that means sharing a bed."

"Yes."

For a moment I wonder if he's lying. Just making it up so he can be in a position to get his groove on with me. But then, that's a huge charade to come up with just for a little booty call. And really, he doesn't seem the type to have to trick his dates into bed, not with his looks and appeal.

"Okay, fine," I say. "We'll share a room."

"I can sleep on the floor," he volunteers, going all knight-in-shining-armor chivalrous again.

I shake my head. "I appreciate the gesture, but there's no need." I gesture to the bed. "It's like king-sized plus. I'm sure we can both fit comfortably on it."

"Okay. If you're sure."

"Yup. Positive. And speaking of beds . . ." Even though I just woke up a short time ago, I already feel sleepy again. I kick off my shoes and crawl under the covers on the left side of the bed.

In turn, Magnus pulls off his shirt, revealing those killer abs that make me drool every time, then joins me in bed, keeping his distance on the right side.

So now we're in the same bed, but chasms apart. And while I freely admit I've never shared a bed with a guy, even platonically, it doesn't seem that weird. And I completely trust Magnus, for some unknown reason, not to do any funny business.

"Get some rest," the vampire says, turning over to his side to face me. "We're going to have a busy night tonight finding the Grail."

"I will," I say, yawning. I cuddle into my plush feather pillow. This bed is truly deluxe and I feel suddenly very warm and safe. "Thanks."

"You're welcome," he says simply. Then he smiles a sleepy little smile and my insides involuntarily go to mush. "I am happy to do it."

"No, I mean for everything," I babble on, not quite ready to shut my eyes for some reason. Not quite ready to stop looking into his beautiful blue eyes, if we're being completely honest here. "You've got a ton on your plate with the whole taking over the coven thing. And bringing me here to England on what could be a total wild goose chase is probably the last thing you wanted to do this week."

He reaches over and brushes a strand of hair from my eyes. "It's no bother. Really."

"You know, Magnus," I say, feeling warm and cozy from his touch and for once deciding not to fight the tingly feelings. "You're really a nice guy. If I *did* want to be a vampire, you'd totally be my first choice for blood mate."

He smiles again, though this time I'm half convinced his eyes look a little sad. "Go to sleep, Sunny," he whispers, leaning over to kiss me softly on the forehead. "Go to sleep."

I do.

20

A Rave Mistake

I sleep like a rock and wake on my own when the sun sets, feeling well rested, though ravenously hungry. I open my eyes. Somehow in the middle of the day, Magnus has shifted in his sleep and is currently lying with his arm draped over me, spooning me into him. Surprised at the nearness and more than a bit uncomfortable, I squirm out of bed, waking him in the process.

He rubs his eyes sleepily. "Is it nighttime?" he asks.

I glance at the bedside clock. "Yup. Eight P.M. on the dot." I wonder if he has any idea I was just in his arms. Hopefully not, as that would be *très* awkward.

"Excellent." He rises from bed and grabs his shirt from the floor, pulling it over his head. "Time to head to Glastonbury."

Since we've both slept in our clothes, there's not much getting-ready time and moments later I follow him out of the bedroom and down the stairs.

"What's Glastonbury like, anyhow?" I ask as we step outside the mansion. The limo is still waiting for us, go figure. I wonder if the driver got any sleep.

"It's a very quiet village, home to many artisans and spiritualists," Magnus explains as we get into the limo. "Quaint, actually. A pleasant holiday spot for most tourists."

"Cool." I always wanted to visit one of those stereotypical English country towns, with stone cottages and antique shops.

"Once a year they have a major festival with big-name musical acts," he continues. "The crowds descend on the town in droves. Usually more than a hundred thousand people show up, if you can believe it. They camp for three days in a field, listen to music, dance, and do God knows what drugs. It's meant to be quite insane."

"Sounds cool. When's the festival?"

"Oh, they don't hold it until the end of June or so. Never in May."

I frown, disappointed. "Too bad. It sounds like a blast."

"Believe me, it's for the best. With a hundred thousand people crowding the town, the druid order makes itself scarce. We'd never find them and thus never find the Grail."

"Oh. Well, then I guess it's a good thing it's not that time of year." Obviously, getting the Grail is much more important than partying at some big English rave.

"Indeed."

"Still, it would have been kind of cool to see. A hundred thousand people standing in a field, all one with the music. You don't get that in America."

Magnus pauses for a moment, then says, "If you really want to see it, I can take you in June, if you like."

I glance over at him, completely taken aback. Is he making postvampire plans with me? Does he honestly think we'll be hanging out with each other after I turn back into a human? Is it even possible to keep some kind of relationship . . . friendship going between a vampire and a human? And if it is possible, is that what I want to do?

Do I want to keep hanging out with Magnus after I've been rehumanized? I've only known him a few short nights, but if I'm being completely honest here, I do kinda like having him around. He's funny and interesting and loyal and chivalrous, and yummy as anything. What's not to like? Then again, what will I do when he eventually gets assigned another blood mate? Will he drop me like a hot clove of garlic when the Council assigns him a real, willing partner? His true queen? And how will I deal with that?

No, I decide to myself. It's better to make a clean break of it. Once I turn back into a human, that's it. I'm severing all ties. Forgetting vampires even exist and going on with my normal boring everyday life.

"Um, Sunny? You know what I was just saying about taking you to the festival?" Magnus says, interrupting my whirling thoughts. I glance over. He's staring out the tinted window.

Okay, here goes. Time to make the break. I swallow hard. "You know, Mag, you really don't have to—"

"I think we may see it after all."

"Huh?"

Magnus leans back into his seat. "Look out the window."

I scramble over him to cup my hands over the glass and peer outside. Then I gasp.

The festival, it seems, has been moved up a month.

Everywhere I look, there's people. All types of people. Young people. Old people. People with dreadlocks. People with mohawks. People dressed in designer clothes and people dressed as Goths. Hippies, ravers, stoners, metalheads. All swarming the streets with sloshy plastic cups of beer.

"Oh my gosh," I cry. "The festival is . . . now?" The second I voice the question I realize how obvious the answer is. We're in the middle of a swarm of people.

I sink back into the leather seat. Great. Just great. I make it all the way to England and it just happens to be on the one day of the year when the druids I'm seeking go into hiding. Once again, my lack of luck astounds me.

"Wow. This sucks," I say mournfully.

"Indeed," Magnus agrees, as always not the most optimistic of blood mates.

"What are we gonna do?"

"Well, there's no way to find the druids in this mess," he

says, peering out the window again. "They'll have gone underground. We'll just have to wait it out."

"But it's Thursday night. And I turn into a vampire on Saturday. That doesn't give us much time."

Magnus reaches over and squeezes my knee. I know he means it to be comforting, but it's totally not. "I know, Sun," he says. "It's a complete disaster. I'm so sorry."

I look out the window again, feeling the tears well up in my eyes and drip down my cheeks. Of all the unfortunate things to happen, this has got to be the worst. My one chance for redemption has been ruined by a massive flock of English raver kids. Don't they have school? Don't they have lives? Why are they here, set on ruining mine?

I try to resign myself to life as a vampire. It won't be that bad, will it? I mean, I'll have riches beyond my wildest belief, unimaginable powers. That'll be fun, right? And hey, if we're being honest here, sunshine is completely overrated. As is college. And getting married and having a family. And . . .

Oh, what's the use? No matter how you slice it, this absolutely blows. I don't want to be a vampire. I'm sure it's a fine lifestyle choice for some people. But it's just not me.

The sobs come in full force now. Choking, rasping gulps of sorrow that rack my body. Soon, I'm crying so bad I'm actually shaking. All this time I've held out hope that somehow the process could be reversed. And now that I know I'm doomed, the magnitude of my situation hits me like some Acme anvil in a Road Runner cartoon.

This sucks.

This totally sucks.

This totally, utterly, and unbelievably sucks.

Suddenly I feel arms around me, pulling me away from my dark pit of despair and enveloping me in a warm, safe embrace. I press my head against Magnus's shoulder and just let him hold me as I cry. Let him stroke my back with his fingers as I choke out my sobs.

"Shh, shh," he soothes. "It's going to be okay."

"It's *not* going to be okay," I cry. "I'm going to be a vampire forever."

"That's not necessarily true," he whispers. "We can find a way. Or wait till the festival is over. The place could be completely evacuated tomorrow, which would give us plenty of time to find the Grail."

I sniff, wishing I had a Kleenex to wipe my nose. I hate getting all slobbery like this. I pull away from Magnus's hug, so I can look him in the eyes. He gazes back at me, solemn and concerned.

"You really think we have a chance?" I ask, brushing the tears away with my sleeve.

He nods slowly. "I do," he says. "And Sunny, I don't want to sound negative here, but even if we don't, which I don't think will happen," he adds, probably in response to my crumpling face, "but worst-case scenario," he reaches over and cups my face in his hands. I suck in a breath. "I want you to know that I won't abandon you. I won't leave you to fend for yourself. If you have to stay a vampire, I promise you now, I will be your blood mate in every sense of the word. As long as you want me or need me, I will keep you safe. You don't have to be afraid. I will never leave you."

This promise, this confession, this ultimatum from the beautiful creature in front of me is almost too much. My heart breaks and soars all at the same time. I don't know whether to throw up or throw my arms around him.

"Th-thank you," I murmur. "That means a lot to me."

He doesn't reply. Well, not with words anyway. He just leans in and kisses me.

21

He Did the Mash.
He Did the Monster Mash

It isn't like our first kiss, the one out in the parking lot of Club Fang. That was a kiss full of lust. Of empty passion between two strangers who knew nothing of one another. And it isn't like the kiss Jake Wilder gave me just before I jetted off to England. That was, admittedly, a bit on the sloppy side.

This kiss is different. It's impossible to describe. At least not without sounding like someone out of my Aunt Edna's romance novels.

So I stay still for a moment, simply enjoying the softness of his lips moving against mine, forgetting for a moment all my pain, my worries, my fears, and just relaxing into his embrace. Taking in the strength and reassurance his mouth is offering me. (Okay, maybe I *am* stepping into romance heroine-speak for a moment, so sue me.)

And then, against my better judgment, I kiss him back.

For a moment, we are one. Tasting, touching, loving one another. There are no longer human-vampire cohabitation issues. Just two individuals who feel the undeniable need to connect with one another on a kind of base, intimate level.

Insert major dreamy sigh here.

He pulls away first, blushing furiously. I notice blood tears leaking from the corners of his eyes before he brushes them away.

"I'm sorry," he mutters, turning to look out the window. "I shouldn't have done that."

I stare at him for a moment, unable to speak, knowing that whatever I say next will turn the tide of our relationship forever. I realize my fingers are clawing at the leather seats and I release my hold.

I think of the possibilities. If I stay vampire, there's no reason we can't hook up, right? I mean, we're blood mates; our DNA is compatible to spend an eternity with one another. And after all, if I'm stuck as a vamp, there's no one I'd rather be stuck with than sweet, perfect, caring Magnus who kisses like a god.

By the same token, if I do manage to regain my humanity (and let's be honest, that's plan number one), would it be realistically feasible to keep such close ties to an immortal creature of the night?

Seriously. I mean, what would it be like to have a vampire boyfriend? As far as I can imagine, it could never work. We couldn't get married, for one. (What would he put on the marriage license as his date of birth?) And after a few years, I'd start growing old and he'd stay looking like a teenager forever. What would people say to an aging sixty-year-old woman with a handsome teenage boyfriend? (Well, besides "ew" anyway.) I mean, the whole Demi and Ashton thing is weird enough. This would be much, much worse.

And then there's the blood mate issue. The Council will eventually assign Magnus a new, proper blood mate. Someone to spend eternity with who won't grow old and complain about her arthritis. And what am I supposed to do then? Make it a threesome? Somehow I doubt Mrs. New Blood Mate would be down with that.

Nope, there's no way around this. It's not going to work. And it's probably better to pull off the Band-Aid all at once, as they say, rather than slowly prolonging the torture. Stop myself. Stop him. Stop this budding relationship now— before I'm in too deep. Before I find myself in love or something equally ridiculous like that.

"I think we need to concentrate on finding the Grail right now," I say firmly, crossing my arms over my chest. I hope I look confident and in control, 'cause inside all that's raging is doubt and confusion. I hold my breath, waiting for his response. Is he going to be pissed? Or beg me to reconsider?

But all he does is nod and I can see his hard swallow. "Of course," he agrees, clearing his throat. "We should most certainly be concentrating on that."

I squeeze my eyes shut. Gah! This is so, so hard. Suddenly all I want to do is throw my arms around him and continue where we left off. Kiss him senseless all night long. But that would be really stupid. Impulsive gratification that would lead to a lifetime of regret.

I can feel him staring at me, his beautiful blue eyes boring into my skull, as if he's attempting to read my mind. I suddenly realize I never did determine whether he had the power to do that. I hope he doesn't. I don't want him to see all the confusion swirling around in my head.

"Well, since we're here," I say at last, determined to switch to a safer, less painful subject, "maybe we should go out and enjoy the festival."

Magnus glances out the window again, looking as if I just asked him to dine on the blood of a garlic farmer. I don't blame him. I'm sure the last thing he wants to do at this moment is wade through a crowd of drunken revelers, taking in the sights like some undead tourist with nothing better to do.

"Never mind," I say, taking it back. Screw it. I don't want to make things worse. Plus, how much fun could we really have in our depressed, mopey states? "It was a dumb idea."

"No, no," Magnus protests, looking back at me, his expression completely unreadable. "It's a rather good idea, actually.

You'll probably never get a chance to experience such chaos again. Might as well make the most of it, right?" He tries to smile, but it's definitely a halfhearted attempt.

"Okay," I hedge. "If you're sure . . ."

"Sure, I'm sure. It'll be fun."

I'd actually believe him, if he weren't wearing a death-warmed-over expression on his pale face. But before I can object, he instructs the limo driver to wait here and opens the car door.

"Let's go," he says with what sounds to me like forced cheerfulness.

We step out into the night. Into the crowds. Into the craziness. "Here goes nothing," I mutter, not sure why I thought this was a good idea.

We struggle to make our way through the throng, buy two tickets from a bearded scalper wearing a Tottenham Hotspurs soccer jersey. Then we head through the makeshift gates and onto the field. And it's there that my jaw drops open in wonderment.

Wow. All I can say is *wow.*

Seriously, you've never lived until you've seen a hundred thousand people dancing all at once. The stage appears miles away and the performers look like ants from our location. But that doesn't seem to bother the festivalgoers in our geographic sphere. They're dancing like they've got front-row tickets to the action—bouncing up and down to the music, screaming their heads off, and generally having a grand old time.

I grin, feeling my doubt and depression slink away, replaced by a shared vibe of excitement. I mean, how cool is this? We have nothing like it in America. These Brits really know how to rock out. I'm so glad we decided to get out of the car.

"Well, this is a bit disconcerting, isn't it?" Magnus yells in my ear, evidently not sharing my enthusiastic sentiments. Then again, as a proper, thousand-year-old vampire, I'm guessing this mania really isn't his regular scene.

I, on the other hand, have determined that I'm going to have a good time and he's not going to wreck it for me. 'Cause I deserve it, after all I've been through this week. Yup, I'm now ready to cut loose and stop thinking about all the bad stuff and just get down on the dance floor. (Or grass floor, as the case may be.)

And that means Magnus is so not allowed to be the old fuddy-duddy stick in the mud that I can see he's planning to be. We need to put our differences aside tonight. Enjoy ourselves and our unique surroundings. After all, this could be a once-in-a-lifetime experience. I want to enjoy it.

So I grab him by the hand and drag him into the midst of the throng. "Dance!" I yell at him, not sure he can hear me over the music. I start bopping to the beat myself, hoping he'll get the picture.

He rolls his eyes and stands still for a moment, perhaps calculating how many vampire coolness points he'd lose for getting his groove on at the Glastonbury Festival. Knowing what I do about the Vampire Code, I'm sure raving's considered "behavior not becoming" for the incoming king. But still . . .

"There's no one here to see you," I remind him. "And I'll never tell!" I grab his hands and start dancing around him, trying to force him to move. At first he stands there like a stone statue, then slowly starts nodding his head to the beat. Then, other body parts follow.

At first he's awkward, just going through the motions. But by the time the next song starts up, I can tell he's getting into it. By midtune, he's totally boogieing down.

"Whoo-hoo!" I cry, throwing my arms around him in a big hug. I probably shouldn't be doing things like that, seeing as I'm trying to keep our relationship on a platonic level. But at that moment, it feels like a perfectly normal thing to do. And hey, we're still friends, right? And friends hug. No big deal. I squeeze tighter. "I knew you could do it!" I say in his ear.

He laughs. "Bloody hell!"

And so we dance. And hop. And twirl. At one point we dance together, clutching onto one another like deranged prom dates. I can tell from the looks on the other ravers' faces that this kind of twosome "old-fashioned" dancing isn't really festival approved. But I don't care. Having Magnus's hands on my waist, spinning me on the grassy dance floor, feels too good for me to worry about what other people think.

After what seems like hours of cardio, we collapse, laughing and sweaty and exhausted, onto a nearby grassy clearing that is remarkably free of people.

"Whew!" I cry. "That was fun."

"Indeed."

Magnus lies down on the grass, staring up into the darkened sky. I join him. It's a beautiful night. The moon hangs low and full and is almost orange in its intensity. Perfect temperature and a clear sky, glittering with pinpricks of light. Nice. You know, if I do end up stuck as a vampire for all eternity—never again setting foot under the sun—at least I'll always have the stars to keep me company.

"I haven't been dancing in probably eighty years," Magnus admits. "Not since the Roaring Twenties, I shouldn't think."

"Really?" I'm surprised. That's a long time not to get your groove on. "Not even at Club Fang?"

"Not really my thing," he admits. "Just 'cause I'm a vampire, doesn't mean I'm into the Goth scene."

"Yeah. I suppose that makes sense," I reason. "Like why go around dressing in black and wishing you were dead, when technically you already are."

He grins. "Exactly."

"Well, your first time dancing in nearly a century—how did you enjoy it?"

"Very much so. I think I might only wait a decade or two to try it again," he says dryly. I shove him playfully on the shoulder.

"Whatever, dude. We're so dancing again in like five minutes' time and you know it!"

"Are we now? Well, if you say so, it must be true."

I roll onto my side to face him and he does the same. "Come on, admit it. You had fun. You're dying to do it again."

"All right, all right. It was quite enjoyable," he says with a small smile. "But don't say a word to anyone back at the coven. I'm trying to build up credibility for my takeover. And I hardly think 'getting my groove on,' as you so delicately put it, will impress many as to my leadership abilities."

"Who cares what they think? I mean, screw them! What business of theirs is it what you do in your spare time? Are you vamps not allowed to have fun or something?"

He sighs. "Vampire politics are very complicated. And our systems have been in place for nearly a thousand years. Most of our kind are very set in their ways and do not take kindly to modernisms or vampires who try to stay with the times. It's unfortunate, though," he adds after a pause. "I believe our species is missing out on a lot of good nights out."

"Well, when you're king you can change all that."

"It's not that easy. But we shall see." He reaches over and brushes away a lock of hair that's fallen into my sweaty face. I wish he wouldn't keep doing that. I find it way too romantic for comfort. "You have a great outlook on life, Sunny," he says, softly. "I could learn a lot from you."

I can feel myself blushing and have no idea how to respond. "Thanks?" I venture at last.

He smiles, but doesn't speak. For a moment we just stare at one another. I wonder if he's going to kiss me again, but he doesn't make a move. He's probably afraid to, seeing how I reacted the last time. Instead he just lies there and watches me with his sad, blue, beautiful eyes.

I can't stand it.

"I love this song! Let's go dance," I exclaim, jumping to my feet. I don't really love this song. In fact, I'm not even sure what song it is. Or what band, for that matter. But I've got to break the spell somehow and this is the only way I can think to do it.

I grab him by the hand and yank him up. He laughs and together we weave back out into the crowds. Soon we're dancing again and I'm relieved to note that Magnus seems to have abandoned his dark thoughts and looks actually rather happy as he moves to the rhythm of the night.

It seems like only minutes later, but must be hours, when I look up at the sky. The horizon has pinkened with predawn light. "We'd better get going," I tell Magnus. "We don't want to be caught in the sun."

"One more song?" he begs. "I love Oasis."

I laugh. Gone is the cool, slightly ironic vampire he pretends to be. Now he's a kid in a candy store. Eyes shining. Alive. (Well not technically alive, but you know what I mean.) Mission accomplished.

"Fine by me. You're the one who's going to be burned to a crisp," I tease.

He sighs. "You're right, of course. Let's go."

We head back to the limo, which miraculously is still waiting for us. Guess if you pay someone enough, he'll stick around till Judgment Day. So cool. I would love one of these chauffeur setups to bring me to school and back everyday. Fetch my lunch from the local pizza joint and have it hot and waiting for me at lunchtime.

The chauffeur opens the door for us and we climb inside. If I had a limo, though, I'd redo the boring interior. Maybe throw up a few disco lights or something. Make it really fun. Hmm, I wonder if MTV ever pimps these kinds of rides.

The chauffeur gets in his side and puts the key in the ignition. Soon, we're speeding back to Château du Vampire.

"That was so much fun," I say, after a long yawn, sinking back into my leather seat. I'm so sleepy all of a sudden. I guess hours upon hours of dancing in a field will do that to a girl. Not that it wasn't totally worth it.

"Indeed," Magnus agrees. "I had a fantastic time. More fun than I've had in centuries." He smiles his shy smile. "Thank you, Sunny."

"Anything for you, Maggy," I respond, trying to keep the mood light. I can't bear to have him go all mushy again. It'll ruin all my work to keep things platonic.

I close my eyes, pretending to sleep, mainly to avoid looking at him. But even with my eyes squeezed shut, I can feel him on the other side of the limo. His stare. His desire for me. I don't know if it's a blood mate thing or what, but I can feel it radiating from his body.

He wants me. I'm sure of it. As sure as I am about Marshmallow Peeps being the best candy in the universe. And if I'm being completely honest here, I want him, too. In fact, I'd like nothing better than to cuddle up next to him and sleepily exchange sweet kisses and caresses all day long.

But I can't. I can't give in. I must stay strong. Break this all off now, before it's too late. Before I fall in love.

I open one eye and steal a glance over at him. He smiles at me.

Oh God, what if I already have?

22

Ancient Druid or
Mad Football Hooligan?

When I awake that night, it's raining hard. And I can hear the wind whistling through the trees. I climb out of bed, careful not to wake Magnus, and pull back the heavy drapes to look out the window. This is the stereotypical weather everyone says England always has, I guess.

Suddenly I miss America with a vengeance. What am I doing here? In a foreign country, spending the night dancing in a field like a crazy person, with only a vampire to keep me company? This isn't me. I'm normal. Average. I don't do things like this.

I just want to go home.

But I can't. Not until we get the Grail. Otherwise this whole adventure has been for nothing. Otherwise I'll be stuck as abnormal for eternity.

I look at my watch. Eight P.M. I wonder how Rayne is doing, handling Mom. Pretending to be me. She sounded a little bored of the charade when I called her early this morning. But she said not to worry. That she'd take care of everything.

She never stresses out or overthinks anything. She just goes with the flow and doesn't care what people say. I envy that in her.

"Sunny?"

I turn back to the bed. Magnus is sitting up, rubbing his eyes sleepily. Guess I woke him up after all.

"Hey," I say, quickly exchanging my view of him for one of the ground, mainly to avoid seeing him shirtless and sexily mussed from sleep. Seriously, when I wake up in the morning (or evening in this case) I look like death warmed over. He looks like Brad Pitt at the Oscars.

"Hey yourself."

Wow. This is kind of awkward, really. Things still feel so unsettled between us.

"So, um, do you think the festival's over?" I ask, trying to stay on neutral ground.

Magnus nods. "Yes, I heard someone say Oasis was the final act. So I'm sure everyone's either left or is sleeping it off somewhere."

"So do you think that means that the druids could be back then?"

"Hopefully. We shall certainly try to find out."

"Cool. Well, what are we waiting for? Let's go."

Magnus gives me a funny look, but doesn't comment at first. Is it that obvious that I just want to get him dressed and out of the bedroom ASAP?

"Sunny, I think we need to talk," he says at last.

Talk? Sudden panic grips me like a vice. I don't want to talk! If we talk, he's going to tell me something I don't want to hear. Like that he's in love with me. Or that he wants me to stay a vampire with him. And then I'll have to choose. And I don't want to choose. Choosing is so overrated.

I mean, what if I make the wrong choice? Go with my feelings and decide something stupid, like staying vampire forever? Then what if after a few months we start not getting along so well? He's staying out late and partying with the boys. And I'm stuck in the coven kitchen, crying in my bowl of blood. He comes home drunk and tells me that his feelings have changed. "It's not you, it's me," he'll say lamely. And then he'll leave again. And I'll be stuck, alone. A vampire without a blood mate. And I'll wish I'd never given in and sacrificed my humanity, all because I thought a vampire looked yummy without his shirt on.

Okay, I'm projecting a bit here, but you get the point.

"Can't we talk later?" I plead. "I really want to see about getting the Grail first."

Magnus's face falls. I can see his disappointment clearly. But all he does is nod. "Fine," is his single-word answer.

He gets out of bed, slamming things around as he gets dressed. Letting me know, in not so many words, that he's ticked off about my avoidance issues.

Well, tough. He'll have to deal. I need that Grail blood. That's my number one priority right now. Relationship talks can come later.

Soon, after showering and dining (don't ask, I don't want to talk about it!) we find ourselves once again making our way to Glastonbury in a speeding limo driving on the wrong side of the street. We're both silent. Both staring out the windows to avoid looking at one another.

We approach the town limits. This time, however, there are no roadblocks or crazy drunken teens to keep us from our mission. This time we can drive right up to the main street of the once-again sleepy little hillside town.

We step out of the limo and instruct the ever-patient driver to wait. I look around. The place is utterly charming— your stereotypical little English village with pubs and art galleries and cozy tea shops that are spelled *shoppe*. Of course, everything's closed for the night (except the pubs, which are packed with locals, most likely celebrating the fact that the damned festival is over for another year).

I whirl around, taking it all in. "This is so adorable! I love quaint little towns like this." I peer into a darkened window. "It'd be so cool to come here in the day and really explore the place."

"Well, if we don't get moving, you won't have that luxury ever again," Magnus reminds me in a completely unwarranted grumpy tone. Ugh. What crawled up his butt and died?

"Okay, okay," I say, abandoning the shop window to follow him down the road, which is lined by tall, skinny townhouses. "Where are we going, anyhow?"

"Here," Magnus says, stopping abruptly in front of one of the nondescript townhouse doors.

"Here? How do you know it's here?" I scratch my head. "It looks like every other house we've just passed."

Magnus points to the brass knocker on the door. "The door bears the sign of the goddess," he informs me. "Druids live here."

"Oh. Okay." *Just shut up, go along, and don't ask dumb questions, Sunny.* "So are we going to just knock and ask whoever comes to the door about the Grail? Do you think they'll know? Do you think they'll tell us if they do?"

Magnus gives me a look. Shut up. Dumb questions. Right. I'll just go check out this lovely flower box.

The vampire grabs the brass knocker and taps out a couple of short, then long knocks. I want to ask him if it's some secret druid code he's tapping, but I've learned my lesson on the dumb questions thing.

Moments later the door creaks open and a wizened old man with a long gray beard sticks his head out. I stare at him. He looks exactly like Gandalf the Grey of *Lord of the Rings*

fame. How cool is that? Finally, after the disappointing images of the Slayer and the vampire leader Lucifent, someone
who actually looks the part.

"Can I help you?" he asks in a deep, rumbly English voice.

"We seek audience with the Pendragon," Magnus answers. "Can you help us?"

Gandalf's eyes narrow. "What would one such as yourself
seek with our Order? You are not of this world."

Wow. He can tell that just by looking at Magnus? I wish
I'd had that ability when I first met the guy. Then I wouldn't
be in all this mess.

Magnus bows his head low. "I am quite aware that I am a
damned creature of the night, my lord. However, I have a
great need that I hope can be addressed. And may I remind
you, 'tis not the first time our two faiths have joined one another in noble purpose."

"You speak true." Gandalf opens the door wide. "Step inside, my son."

Hmm. So the druids and the vamps have hooked up in the
past? I wonder what that was about? I mean, you've got your
druids, who are nature-loving tree huggers. Then you've got
your vampires, who like to drink blood and lavish themselves
in luxurious underground palaces. Not a big common bond,
as far as I can see. But hey, what do I know?

We step inside the house and walk down a narrow corridor and into a quaint little parlor. Gandalf (who introduces

himself as Llewellyn the Pendragon, which is evidently some kind of leadership position in the druid world) invites us to sit down and asks if we'd like a "spot o' tea."

"Though I understand it is not your drink of choice," he says to me with a wink. Ugh. Grandpa Druid isn't trying to hit on me, is he?

After we tell him we're cool with the whole tea thing and would just prefer to get down to business, the old druid sinks into one of the parlor chairs and leans forward, elbows on his knees, saying he's eager to hear our request.

So Magnus goes through the whole spiel. My accidental bite. How he's been trying to reverse the transformation. How only a drop of pure blood from the Holy Grail can do the trick, yada, yada, yada.

"I see," Llewellyn says when he's finished. "And you are under the impression that we know where the Grail is buried."

"I had hoped," Magnus agrees, "that you would be so kind as to lead us there."

"We have been chosen by the Goddess herself to be the Guardians of the Grail for millennia," Llewellyn says, his voice cold and formal. "'Tis a task we take seriously. Allowing an unpure, undead being near the holy chalice would be blasphemy."

My heart sinks at his words. Oh great. He's going to be difficult about this, isn't he? Figures. We get this far and then we're totally shot down. I just know I am doomed to walk the earth as an undead forever. Perfect.

"I understand," Magnus says. "Though perhaps a tithe, made to the Goddess, the great Earth Mother, would ease her mind about such a trespass."

Llewellyn frowns. "Do you dare bribe me, vampire?" he asks, angrily. "You should know better than that. Our Order is based on love and nature and purity. We are not mercenaries, able to be bought with something as common as coin."

"A tithe of one million pounds," Magnus adds in an even voice.

My mouth drops open. So does Llewellyn's, though he quickly shuts it again.

"Let me . . ." He clears his throat. "Let me consult with the Goddess in our Sacred Grove. I shall return with your answer."

He rises from his seat and exits the room. Once he's gone, Magnus turns to me.

"Lesson number one. Everyone has their price," he says. "Even those who commune with nature must still pay rent and buy food at the market."

I giggle. "But a million pounds, Mag?" I ask, remembering the amount he offered. "That's a lot of money. Almost two million American dollars if I've got the conversion right. Are you sure you want to give a million pounds?"

"You are worth it."

Gah. What do I even say to that? I can't deal when he says stuff like that. I mean, in one sense I like it. It gives me that whole chills-tripping-down-my-spine thing. But in another, I realize it's dangerous. I can't succumb to his charm. I must move on with my life.

"Yeah, yeah," I reply at last, using sarcasm to deflect his sentiments. "Whatever."

Eager to change the subject, I bounce up from my seat and head over to the door that Llewellyn has just exited. I put my ear to the wood. (Aren't druids supposed to be one with the trees and thus against objects created through their demise, like wooden doors? It'd be like a Hindu chowing on cow or my vegetarian mom wearing leather pumps.)

"It's a million pounds, dude!" a voice on the other side is saying. A voice, in fact, that sounds remarkably like Llewellyn's, were he to use words like *dude*, which before now I would not have guessed him to do. "Is that bleeding fantastic or wot?"

"Yeah, but wot we're supposed to be is Guardians and stuff," another male voice argues. "You know. Sacred Mission and all that?"

"Eff that, mate. Do you know what kind of flat in London we could get for a million pounds? We could spend every night at the pub downing Stella, watching footy on the telly, and picking up fancy birds. It'll be brilliant."

Hm, somehow I'm thinking he's not talking about blue-jays and robins here. So much for Nature Boy and his Holy Orders. I'm actually a bit disappointed. But if I've learned one thing on this crazy vampire journey, it's that no one is really like you'd imagine them to be. And, of course, in this case, the old leader of an ancient druid order turning out to be a money-grubbing hooligan greatly works out to our benefit.

"A'right," the other voice agrees. "But let's show 'em the Grail real quick. In-and-out like, before the rest of 'em wake up from their festival 'angovers and we have to share the quid with those tossers."

"Too right."

I leap back to my seat, just in time for "Llewellyn" (BTW I'm pretty convinced now that's a fake name; he's probably really called Bob or something) to walk through the door in the most regal, ceremonial manner. Heh.

"Good people of the earth," he begins, back to speaking like he's a cast member from *Lord of the Rings*. "I have returned from my consultation with the Good Mother, who once bore the very earth from her womb."

I stifle a giggle. Yeah. Good Mother, a.k.a Cockney friend in the kitchen, same diff.

"And?" Magnus prompts.

"And she has—" He pauses for dramatic effect. Honestly, these druids are almost as bad as the Goths. "—decided to grant your request. On the account that your mission is to purify and redeem the blood of a virgin who has been cruelly ripped from innocence by a damned creature of the Other World."

Okay, I know his speech is total BS, but excuse me, how the hell does everyone know that I'm still a virgin? Really, I want to know. Is there some stamp on my forehead I can't see? Some secret handshake I don't know?

"Please tell the Good Mother that we are eternally grateful for her extreme generosity," Magnus instructs, before I can tell the druid to stop casually throwing around the V-word. The vampire holds out a briefcase I hadn't noticed him carrying. "And that I hope this tithe will further the good work that she pursues."

Or allow two local guys to drink and get laid, in this case, but hey, it all works for me.

Llewellyn accepts the briefcase, his eyes shining with his greed, and opens it. Inside lie stacks upon stacks of high-numbered bills.

"Holy fu—" he starts, then catches himself. "Yes, this tithe will be most pleasing to Her Goodness." He closes the briefcase and tells us he will return. Then he exits back into the kitchen.

Magnus and I exchange amused glances. "I still think he would have taken much less of a . . . donation," I say.

The vampire shrugs. "I would have given him much more."

I blush again. He's been so good to me. "Thank you, Mag," I say. "It really means a lot to me."

"I know," he says in a very serious tone. "It means a lot to me as well."

23

Grail Hunting

About fifteen minutes later we're climbing down a dark spiral stone staircase, deep underground, with Llewellyn as our guide. Still holding on to that false nature image, he insists on using a torch to light our way. But whatever. As long as we get there, I guess.

"This passageway leads underneath the mighty Tor," our druidic tour guide explains. "It was dug a thousand years ago by our Order's ancestors."

Wow. Real fascinating. You know, this guy could get a job as a tour guide for the Tower of London, once he blows his million on booze and chicks.

We reach the bottom of the stairs and come to a wrought-iron gate. Llewellyn reaches into his robe to pull out an antique-looking key, made of gold. No high-tech key codes for these guys, I guess. He fits the key into the lock and the gate creaks open, revealing a low ceiling over a cobwebbed passageway, leading into the darkness.

In other words, my worst nightmare.

"This way," Llewellyn commands, beckoning with a long-fingernailed hand.

I stare down the passageway, trying to control my breathing. I'd kind of forgotten how claustrophobic I am. My heart starts pounding in my chest as I watch the torchlight dance off the low-hanging earthen walls. I'd give my left arm, firstborn—anything—if only I could get a halogen headlamp or something.

"It's okay," Magnus whispers in my ear. He grabs my trembling hand. "Relax."

Easy for him to say. Harder for me to do as the walls seem to close in around me. My mind plays out scenarios of earthquakes and floods and other natural disasters that could cause the tunnel to collapse and bury us alive.

I realize I'm digging my nails into Magnus's palm and I loosen my hold. "Sorry," I whisper.

"It is said that Joseph of Arimathea once traveled these passages," Tour Guide Llewellyn presses on, completely oblivious to my stress. "Wanting to discover a safe place to store the cup of his cousin, Jesus Christ, whose blood he had collected as he lay dying on the cross. He felt that blood this pure and holy could be put to good use someday."

"Good thinking, Joey my boy," I mutter.

"He did not feel that, with the persecution of the Christians in the eastern lands, the artifact would be safe. So he entrusted it to our Order. And we have guarded it since."

Yeah, until today, when you sold out poor Joey for a million bucks.

"The cup itself is affixed to a massive stone and cannot be moved. But I have prepared two vials made out of the purest crystal, for you to fill."

"You must wait for Saturday night to actually drink," Magnus whispers. "According to what I have read."

Darn. So it's not an instant reverse-o-matic kind of thing. Figures. But still, I finally have hope. And that's what's important.

We reach a massive door made out of stone. Using another ancient-looking key, Llewellyn unlocks it and the door swings silently open.

We step inside and I draw in my breath, all thoughts of claustrophobia disappearing in an instant.

I don't know how many of you have seen *Indiana Jones and the Last Crusade*, but in that movie, he gets to the room where the Holy Grail is stored and there are a million different ornate cups and he has to figure out which one is the real one, 'cause if he drinks from the wrong one he'll die. And it turns out to be the plainest cup of them all.

Well, let me tell you, that's just another one of Hollywood's misconceptions.

For one thing, the room we enter appears to be made entirely of gold. Gold floor. Gold ceiling. Gold walls. And there's only one cup. One Holy Grail. And it's certainly not plain by any stretch of the imagination. It sits front and center, affixed to a massive boulder as Llewellyn mentioned, and is the most ornate cup I've ever laid eyes on. It's gold. There are jewels affixed to it. It's darn fancy, this Holy Grail.

"The Grail," Llewellyn says with a flourish of his hand.

I look over to Magnus to voice my excitement. I notice he's suddenly sweating bullets. Actually sweating blood, if you want to be literal about it. He's also breathing hard and his face is corpse white.

"Are you okay?" I ask. I haven't seen him this affected since I teased him with the cross the first night—

That's it! Being so close to such a religious artifact must be driving him nuts. Poor guy.

"I'm . . . fine," he says in a tight voice. "Just . . . get . . . the blood."

Llewellyn pulls out two clear vials from a pocket in his robe and walks over to the Grail. Magnus makes a soft choking sound and I reach over to squeeze his hand. If I'd known how much this would bother him, I would have suggested I go alone.

I turn back to Llewellyn and watch him dip the vials into

the cup, filling them with a dark, crimson liquid. Then he seals each vial and hands one to me and the other to Magnus.

"Wait, Magnus can't—" I start. I don't want the vial to burn his hand or something.

"I'm fine, Sunny," Magnus says, accepting the vial. "It's sealed."

Oh. Well, who knew? I turn the vial in my hand. "This thing isn't very breakable, is it?" I ask. "'Cause it would suck to get all the way home and have some kind of carry-on luggage accident."

Llewellyn shakes his head. "It is made of crystal and is thick and strong. However, I gave each of you a vial, in case some unfortunate incident should occur."

Well, that was nice of him to think of a contingency plan. But hey, we just gave the guy a million pounds, so we should be expecting good service, I suppose.

"Great." I stuff the vial in my shirt pocket. "Then are we all set here?" I take one last look at the Grail, wishing I'd brought my camera phone. I could have sold the photo to some museum and recouped the million we spent. Um, that Magnus spent, anyhow.

"Come, let us leave the sacred place," Llewellyn says, heading to the door. "It looks as if it is causing your friend much pain."

He's right. Poor Magnus. We should get the hell out of here ASAP before the guy has a seizure or something. So I follow

Llewellyn out and we head back through the passageway. I realize my heart is pounding again. But this time, it's not pounding with claustrophobic fear. This time it's pounding with joy.

"We did it!" I whisper to Magnus, reaching over to give him a hug. "I'm going to get to be human again!"

So why doesn't the vampire look very happy?

24

Thanks for the Memories

The trip back to the good old U. S. of A. is uneventful. In fact, I sleep most of the time, waking only as the plane touches down. I'd have probably even slept longer if Magnus hadn't roused me and urged me to hurry.

"There was some stormy weather over the Atlantic," he explains. "Which made the trip longer than usual. We have little time before the sun comes up to get home."

I nod as I rub the sleep out of my eyes. "Okay," I agree.

Magnus hands me a squeeze bottle. "Breakfast," he says. "For here or to go."

I accept the bottle with a laugh. "You forgot to ask if I'd like fries with that."

He smiles and motions for me to follow him out of the plane. I do and soon we're in his deluxe Jag, zooming through the predawn streets towards my house.

He's quiet during the drive. I feel like I should say something, but I'm not sure what.

"Thanks for helping me get the Grail blood," I say at last. I've already thanked him like a million times, but I am truly grateful for his help, so I guess once more can't hurt. I certainly couldn't have done it without him. Getting to England would have been difficult enough. Coughing up nearly two mil to offer to a football- and beer-loving druid would have been utterly impossible.

"Not a problem," he replies, concentrating on the road in front of him instead of me. I notice his hands are gripping the steering wheel just a tad too tightly and I wonder what's up. But before I can ask, he pulls up in front of my house.

"So, um, I'm supposed to drink this tomorrow?" I ask, rummaging through my jacket pocket for the vial. I turn it over in my hands, admiring the way the crystal catches the Jag's dashboard lights and sparkles.

Magnus nods. "I can meet you somewhere, if you want. To be with you when you drink," he adds. "It's probably going to be a bit . . . disconcerting to change back. I could help you through the discomfort."

"Sure," I say immediately. That's so nice of him to offer. Then I remember. "Oh wait." Damn it. "I'm actually going to be . . . at the prom," I finish lamely.

Magnus raises an eyebrow. "You're still planning on going to the prom?"

"Well, yeah." I shrug. "I mean, I can always drink the blood in the bathroom or something. Or maybe spike my cup of punch?"

"I just figured . . ." Magnus starts then trails off.

"What?"

"Well, it being your last night as a vampire and all . . ."

My heart aches as I realize what he's implying. He wanted to hang out. Spend one last night with me. But while I'd love nothing more, I have to stay strong. Break this off now. Get back to my real life as a human. Go on my date with real-life Jake Wilder and forget my vampire blood mate ever existed.

"Sorry, Mag," I say, trying to sound like I don't care at all, even though nothing is further from the truth. Still, I figure it'll be easier for him to deal with that way. "I've got a date and I can't break it. It's with Jake Wilder, this guy I've had a crush on for like a millennium. One of the most popular boys in school. I can't exactly back out now. It'd be social suicide."

Magnus's face falls. He looks absolutely crushed. I'm a bit surprised. I mean, I knew we shared time together and a hot kiss, but could he really be that attached to me? Could he really feel as strongly about me as I do about him? I remember suddenly that he had wanted to talk and I'd never given him a chance to say what he wanted to say.

I shake my head. Too late now. It doesn't matter. Very soon, I'm going to be a human again. And once I'm a human, there's no point in continuing a romance with a thousand-year-old vampire. I must sever ties now, once and for all, and get on with my human life. A life that will hopefully include hooking up with the luscious Jake Wilder.

So why do I feel so reluctant to do this? Why does my heart suddenly feel like it's being squeezed in a vise?

"Look, Mag," I say firmly, pushing all the doubts out of my head. "I really do appreciate all the help you've given me this last week. But it's time for me to move on. I've got a life. A human life. I can't be chilling with the undead once I get back to normal. Let's be realistic here. We both know this will probably be the last time I ever see you. So thanks for the memories and I wish you well with getting a new blood mate and all."

Ugh. I sound so cold. So mean. So not me. But what else can I say? *Oh, Magnus, I love you so much and my heart is breaking inside*? No. Because then he might ask me to stay. To remain a vampire forever. And I can't make that choice.

"The . . . sun's coming out," he says at last, his face hardening into a mask of indifference. "I've got to go. So, if you don't mind exiting the vehicle . . . ?"

"Oh." Pain stabs at my heart. Was I secretly wishing he wouldn't buy my words? That he'd say, "No Sunny, I can read your mind and I know you really love me and therefore I refuse to let you go." That's ridiculous. I don't want him to say that. I want him to let me go. Right?

I can feel the tears well up behind my eyes. A dam ready

to burst. So without another word, I open the door and get out of the car. I don't turn back to look at him. I don't say good-bye. Because if I did, I know I'd never be able to walk away.

Instead, I run into the house like a coward, not turning around until I'm safely inside. Peering out the window, I watch his car peel out of the driveway and speed off into the dawn.

Then I burst into tears.

25

Twin Sisters Suck

"So did you get it?"

I whirl around, my heart jumping to my throat at the sound of the voice behind me. I'd been so wrapped up in my tortured thoughts and tears that I hadn't heard Rayne approach.

"Sunny?" she says, looking concerned. "Are you okay?"

I nod, unable to speak without choking on the sobs stuck in my throat.

"You didn't get the Grail, did you?" Rayne concludes. "Oh, Sunny, I'm so sorry. I know how much you were counting on that." She approaches me, arms outstretched, inviting me into a sisterly hug. "But really, being a vampire won't be as bad as you think. And I'll help you every step of the way."

I shake my head. "You . . . don't understand," I manage to say. "I got the blood from the Grail."

Rayne drops her arms and looks at me quizzically. "You did?" she asks. "You really got it?"

I pull the vial from my pocket and hold it up for her observation. "I really got it."

"That's great! I'm so happy for you! You must be thrilled." She studies my face. "Though you don't look thrilled. You look, I don't know, like you've lost your best friend or something."

I shrug. "I'm fine."

"And you're crying."

"I'm not."

"Sunny, you're a vampire. You cry blood tears. Not exactly subtle."

I put a hand to my face and then look at it. Sure enough, it's stained red. Ew.

"Okay, so I'm crying. Tears of joy, probably."

"Yeah, right. You think I just fell off the naive truck? I'm your twin sister, remember? Psychic connection and all that. So come on, spill. What's wrong?"

"You're going to think I'm being really, really stupid."

"That's never stopped you from telling me stuff before," Rayne quips. I glare at her. "Sorry. Come on, try me. I promise I won't think you're being stupid."

"Well . . ." I glance out the window again, at the empty driveway where Magnus's car had sat just moments before. "Don't get me wrong. I do want to turn back into a human . . ."

"But?" Rayne prompts.

"But . . ." I start, then burst into another set of tears.

"But you're in love with Magnus," Rayne says somberly.

I stare at her. "How did you . . . ?"

"Call it intuition, I guess. Or that psychic twin link thing I mentioned. Or maybe it's just that you're so freaking obvious about it. In fact, I think even a trained monkey could pick up on your heartbreak vibes right about now. Maybe even an untrained one."

"Oh, Rayne, it's terrible," I cry, ready to let it all out. "I love him. I really do. He's sweet and nice and chivalrous and sexy and funny and I just love him to death." I sniff back my sobs. "Um, no pun intended."

"None taken." Rayne nods. "And all true. So what's the problem?"

"That he's a vampire, duh. And after tomorrow night I'll be a human." I rub my eyes with my fists, wishing I had some tissues.

"Sunny, don't take this the wrong way or anything, but . . ." Rayne pauses for a moment, as if carefully choosing her words. "Did you ever consider . . . not going through with the change? Remaining a vampire so you can be with Magnus?"

"No. No way. I don't want to be a vampire."

Even if it means spending eternity with the guy you're in love with? a voice in my head asks. I shake it away.

"Are you sure?" Rayne presses. Unfortunately, unlike the voices in my head, I can't shut her up as easily.

"Yes. I am sure. Very sure."

I'm not sure at all.

"There are lots of benefits to being a vampire, you know," Rayne says, continuing her pitch, undeterred by my half-hearted assurance. For a moment I wonder why she cares so much. I mean, since when did it matter to her whether I'm undead or alive? Rayne usually cares about nothing but herself. And I know she wants Magnus as a blood mate, so what does it benefit her that we stay together? Weird.

"Riches beyond belief . . ." she drones on.

Maybe she figures if I stay a vampire then she'll have this "in" in the vamp world. Especially since my blood mate is the new king and all. Maybe she figures she'll be able to cut in line, get on the short list to be assigned a new blood mate. That has to be it. There's no other reason she'd be trying to talk me into staying a vampire.

Anger wells up in the pit of my stomach and starts traveling up my throat. She's so selfish. She cares nothing about me and my wants. My dreams and hopes and fears and future. She is simply thinking of herself and what would most benefit her.

"Magical powers . . ." she adds to her list of Top Ten Reasons Sunny Should Stay a Vamp.

Bitch.

Total bitch.

"Freedom to travel anywhere you like. Even Australia . . ."

I can't take it. Not now. Not like this. Next thing you know she's going to bring up her blog again. So help me if she brings up her blog again and the fact that I haven't read it . . .

"If you'd read my blog you'd know that—"

GAH!

"Screw your damn blog, Rayne!" I explode, too furious to worry about waking Mom anymore. "And you know what? Screw you, too. You have no idea what I'm going through. You have some warped notion that this is all fun and games. Well, it's not."

"Sunny—" Rayne tries to interject.

But I'm on a roll and I find I can't stop shouting. "It's not fun to be a vampire. You don't get to see the sun. You don't get to eat garlic-and-chicken pizza. Your mom grounds you because she thinks you're on drugs and you're made to feel bad beyond belief if you have some crazy desire to get your old life back. Well, I refuse to feel guilty for wanting to be a human. For liking the human me and not wanting to sacrifice everything I am to be transformed into some crazy immortal all-powerful being."

I'm raging now. I know I should shut up, but I can't. "Look, Rayne. I want to be a human. I want to have a normal life. I want to go to the prom with Jake Wilder and have a great time with him! I want to dance the night away like a regular high school student and forget this whole mess ever happened.

"I'm sorry if *my* wishes for *my* life don't coincide with yours. I'm sorry if my turning back into a human inconveniences you. But you know what? That's tough luck. This is my life and I'll do whatever the hell I please. So why don't you just eff off and leave me alone!"

Rayne stares at me for a moment, as if she can't believe I just exploded on her. Not surprising since I can't believe it myself. I so didn't mean to go off like that. It just . . . happened.

"Do you have any idea what I've been through, trying to cover for you while you've been gone?" she asks in a tight voice. "Mom practically called out the National Guard when I didn't come home from Spider's for three days. But did I confess? No. I kept up the charade till the bitter end. Now *I'm* the one who's grounded." She turns to stomp off, still muttering under her breath. "Last time I try to help you out, you ungrateful little witch."

Guilt washes over me like a tidal wave. Talk about misplaced aggression. I just completely chewed her out for no reason whatsoever. 'Cause I'm not mad at her, I realize suddenly. I'm mad at myself. And all the stupid decisions I've made.

"Rayne. I'm sorry—" I try.

She whirls around, shooting me daggers with her eyes. "Don't be," she says, her voice cold and venomous. "*I'm* not."

She turns back and starts up the stairs. "Oh and one more thing," she adds, pausing halfway up. "Seeing as you've decided not to stay blood mates with Magnus, you don't mind if I have a go, do you? After all, he was mine first."

My heart sinks to my toes. Could this get any worse? "Sure," I mumble, staring at the ground. "Whatever." What else can I say? I've decided to sever ties with Magnus but I don't want anyone else to date him either? That would be completely unfair. And, as she said, she did have him first.

"Excellent," Rayne says in a triumphant voice as she continues up the stairs. "Thanks, Sun. I can't *wait* to tell him the good news. I'd call him now, but I think it'd be much, much better to meet up face to face. Get him alone and . . . mmmm. De-lish." She grins evilly as she turns the corner and disappears from my line of sight.

I slump into a nearby armchair, sobbing. I try to think about how great it's going to be to return to normal life. How wonderful the prom will be, intimately dancing with Sex God Jake Wilder. Maybe he'll ask me up to his hotel room. Maybe I can shed my Sunny the Innocent cloak once and for all. Maybe he'll fall in love with me and we'll get married and have babies and live happily ever after.

But the fantasy is bittersweet. Because no matter how hard I try, I can't shake the new visions dancing in my head. Rayne hooking up with Magnus. Him kissing her all over and whispering how much he loves her. And for millennia afterward they'll hang out together, drinking blood and talking about the old days. Once in a while they'll bring up that week long ago when he accidentally bit her pathetic twin sister by mistake. Of course, by then I'll be long dead. Worms chewing on my decomposing body.

Oh, what am I going to do?

26

Prom Preparations

"I 'm so glad you're feeling better, sweetie," Mom says, as she fusses over the waffles she's made for me Saturday morning. "I was getting worried about you. But the last few days you seem just like your old self again."

I cringe with guilt. Rayne did such a great job pretending to be me that she got in trouble herself. And what did I do? Rip her a new one because she tried to help. Nice, Sunny.

"Yeah, I feel much better," I say. "Must have gotten over whatever bug I had."

It's true. For some reason, I've suddenly seemed to have lost the creature-of-the-dead crackhead look I started out with and now have this porcelain-doll-of-perfection thing going on. Yup, for the first time in my life, I have absolutely flawless skin. Even my annoying freckles have seemingly faded overnight. Hallelu-jah! That's almost worth remaining a vamp for, in and of itself.

"I'm so glad," Mom says, bringing over a plate of waffles and setting them in front of me. Yuck! Do I have to pretend to eat? I tentatively pick up a fork and pick at the spongy tex-ture. "I didn't want you to miss the prom."

Ah, the prom. I can't believe it's tonight! I don't even have anything to wear! I'll have to hit the mall ASAP.

"Yeah, I can't wait," I say, taking a bite. Bleh. It tastes like cardboard. "Jake's picking me up in a limo."

"Ooh, that's so cool," Mom squeals. Turns out even hippy-dippy save-the-world moms get excited over these silly high school milestones. "You must be really excited."

I nod, trying to look excited, which shouldn't be as hard as it is. After all, going to the prom with the hottest, most popular guy in school is a dream come true, right?

So why am I dreading it so much?

That afternoon I surf the clothing racks at a fancy mall de-partment store, looking for something appropriate for my dream date with Jake. It's funny. A week ago, I'd have told you this was the highlight of my life. Going to the prom. More importantly, going to the prom with a Sex God. But in-stead, I can barely muster up the enthusiasm to try on a gown. And every time I pick one that I think looks halfway decent, I can't help but wonder what Magnus would think of it.

Stop thinking about Magnus, I scold myself for the umpteenth time. It's over. I'm never going to see him again. Well, unless Rayne starts dating him, that is. Then I guess he'll be hanging around a lot. Which is completely fine and doesn't bug me in the least.

Yeah, right.

I finally settle on a pricey black number. Something sexy and slinky and very anti-Sunny. After all, girls who have dates with Sex Gods should look the part. And, a nagging voice in the back of my brain reminds me, on the not-so-remote chance that Jake has only been influenced by my Vampire Scent, once I turn back into a human I'm going to need to impress him. This outfit should do the trick.

I hope.

I bring the dress up to the counter and try to pay the clerk, but he refuses to take my money.

"No, sweetie," he says, handing me back my debit card. "This one's on me."

I should have picked Armani. Taken advantage of the Vampire Scent while I've still got it. If I could keep one vampire power once I turn back, that would be it. So very useful.

I arrive back from the mall with barely enough time to get ready for the event. My mother tells me that Jake's called three times to make sure I'm still going. That I'm still going with him. That I don't mind him picking me up in a limo at seven P.M.

Yes, yes, and yes, though I'm not thrilled by the limo thing, to tell you the truth. It reminds me too much of my mode of transportation while on my recent trip to England. Or, more pointedly, what happened between Magnus and me while we sat in the vehicle in question. But what can you do? I can't exactly tell Jake I'd rather take my mother's Toyota because limos remind me of making out with vampires.

Pathetic, I know.

Once I'm satisfied that my hair and makeup are as good as they're going to get on such short notice, I head back into my bedroom to slip into my dress. Wow. One awesome thing about being a vampire on prom night—flawless figure! Maybe it's due to the fact that I haven't been hungry for human food. Or maybe blood doesn't have a lot of carbs. But for whatever reason, I think I've lost about ten pounds this week. And if you're going to lose ten pounds and then put on a dress, this dress is the one to put on. It molds itself to my body like it was made just for me.

Woot! I'm going to look sooo good.

Seriously. I'm not one for bragging, but as I study myself in the mirror, I realize I'm suddenly superhot. Like Paris Hilton hot, if Paris were five foot four. I just hope I don't turn back into a pumpkin at midnight when I drink the Grail blood. That would royally suck.

* * *

"Done checking yourself out?"

I whirl around. Rayne is standing in the doorway, a scowl on her face.

"Go away," I growl, shooting her a glare before turning back to the mirror. No need for her to ruin what's sure to be the best night of my life.

"Wait. Sunny," she says, ignoring my order and stepping into the room. Gah. I knew I should have installed a lock on my door. "Are you sure you want to go through with this?"

"Go through with what?" I ask. "Going to the prom with Jake? Of course I'm sure. It's what I've dreamed about since I first laid eyes on the guy freshman year."

"No. Not that. The . . . other thing."

"Are you kidding?" I ask, incredulously. I cannot believe that after all of this she's *still* trying to get me to change my mind. As if. "Believe you me, Rayne. I am so ready to skip out on the vampire world. In fact, I wish it were midnight right now. I'd be downing that Grail blood like it's a Cherry Slurpee from 7-Eleven. And you know how I live for Cherry Slurpees from 7-Eleven."

"And what about Magnus?"

My heart sinks. Why did she have to bring up the M-word? I'd never admit it to her, of course, but I've been missing the guy like crazy. Wondering what he's doing. How the coven takeover is going. If they've crowned him king yet. And more important, if they've assigned him a new blood mate. And whether that blood mate happens to be my twin sister.

I know Magnus was mad at my decision to go to the prom, but deep inside, I guess I'd hoped he wouldn't drop off the face of the earth. That he'd still be in my life. I don't know *how* exactly. After all, he's not the type to swing by for tea. Or to call up and ask me out to dinner and a movie or something.

But still . . .

Anyhow, it seems as if that wasn't meant to be. After peeling out of my driveway last night, he's not called or e-mailed or IM'ed or anything. He's just disappeared from my life like he'd never been in it at all.

Not that I mind. I'm glad, actually. It's better this way.

Kind of.

Okay, not really.

"What about Magnus?" I repeat. "Who cares about him?"

I do! I do!

Shut up, heart. You don't count in this case.

"Oh," Rayne replies in an odd voice. In fact, if I didn't know better, I'd think she sounded almost disappointed. Which wouldn't make the least bit of sense, considering she's the one hoping to play Rebound Girl with him. My disinterest should be good news for her. She can have her way with him and live vampily ever after and I won't say a word in objection.

"Okay, then," Rayne adds after a long pause. "If you're sure."

Jeez, what is her problem? "Look, Rayne," I say, a little annoyed, mainly because I have no idea what she's getting at and all this thinking about Magnus is doing nasty things to my insides, "as fascinating as this conversation has been, I'm running a bit late. So if you don't mind, I'd like to cut the chitchat and get ready for my date with the Sex God."

"Oh. I see. Okay. Fine. Whatever." Rayne immediately turns and stomps out of the room.

I turn back to the mirror, feeling a little guilty for being so rude. What's wrong with me lately? She's my twin sister. The person I grew up with. The one who knows me better than anyone.

"Hrmumph," I huff as I pick a stray piece of blond hair off the dress. That just goes to show you. If she knew me better than anyone, she'd know that I'm fully vested into changing back into a human tonight. That I'm in love with Jake Wilder. Not Magnus.

Nope. Rayne doesn't know me at all.

27

Desperate Prom Dates

Jake's prompt. He's rented a limo. And he's dressed in a divine tux. What more could I want in a prom date? He comes to the door and he has a corsage. His cummerbund matches my dress. He smiles at me and calls my mom "ma'am," and he doesn't even bat an eye when she tells him to call her Susan and explains her crazy government conspiracy theory that terms like "ma'am" were put into place to keep women barefoot and pregnant in the kitchen. (Yeah, I don't get her sometimes either.)

In short, Jake is perfect. A dream come true.

So why can't I muster any enthusiasm?

He tells "Susan" he'll have me back at a decent hour. He

allows me to get into the limo first. He offers me a glass of champagne in a fluted glass.

If you looked up *perfect prom date* in the dictionary, Jake's handsome mug would be staring right back at you.

So why am I stifling the urge to yawn?

"To the most beautiful girl at Oakridge High School," he says, as we clink glasses.

"Why are we toasting Mary Markson?" I ask with a giggle.

He scrunches his eyebrows in honest confusion. "I meant you, Sunny," he stammers. "I'm sorry, I guess I should have been more clear."

"Um, I know that," I assure him. "I was just making a joke." A pretty obvious one, I would have thought, but I decide to cut him some slack. I can tell he's nervous. Isn't that too funny? Oakridge High's resident Sex God is nervous around little old me. Who would have thunk it?

I lean back in my seat and take a sip of my champagne. This is nice. Speeding to the prom in a deluxe limo with the most delectable guy in school sitting right across from me. I steal a quick peek. He really is so hot, with those brooding eyes and killer bod. De-lish. And he's all mine.

"I'm so glad you decided to come to the prom with me," Jake continues, giving me a once-over that can only be described as reverent. "I was so scared to ask you."

Imagine! Me scaring a boy! A boy like Jake Wilder scared of me! Too, too funny.

"I'm glad you did," I say, dipping my eyes to appear demure. "I've liked you for a while now."

"Really?" Jake looks surprised. "It's funny, I didn't know you existed until that day in drama."

Ah, there's the icy water of reality dumped on my head. I take a big gulp of champagne, wishing it was blood. I realize I'd been secretly hoping he'd say he'd been lusting after me all year. Then I could report back to Rayne that he really does like me for me and not 'cause of some weird vampire mating call.

But, um, not so much, it appears. Oh well.

"When we were on stage and I kissed you, it was just like my whole world changed in that instant. Everything I was, everything I wanted from life—all disappeared in a flash of light. At that moment, I realized that I could easily spend all eternity with you."

O-kay then. This is getting a bit on the creepy, stalkerish side, I have to admit. I mean, don't get me wrong—having the love of my life spout sonnets of devotion to me while drinking champagne in a luxury limo is extremely cool and all. But knowing he's only doing it 'cause I've inadvertently bewitched him kind of sucks.

I ask you: Is it so hard for a boy to like me for me? To adore and speak passionately about the real life Sunshine McDonald, not her vampire alter ego?

You mean like Magnus does? that annoying voice in my

head asks. *The one guy you know is not influenced by the Vampire Scent?*

No. Not like Magnus, I tell the stupid voice. I really hope it goes away with the rest of the vampire stuff. *I want a human boy to feel that way about me.*

Jake reaches over and starts stroking my knee. "Did I mention how beautiful you are?" he asks.

I stifle another yawn. This is going to be a long night.

We arrive at the prom and parade around the parking lot so all the parents, who evidently have nothing better to do and a lot of film to waste, can clap and cheer and take photo after photo. Of course when they get to me, it's worse. All these balding, potbellied dads start giving me lecherous grins and making "whoo-whoo" noises, much to the chagrin of their wives.

Major ew-age. The heck with free clothes; now that I've got old men leering at me, I'm thinking this Vampire Scent thing has got to go.

After the processional, we walk into the hotel that is hosting the prom. It's pretty nice. Gold-accented walls, crystal chandeliers hanging from the ceiling, and a huge dance floor. On stage there's a DJ spinning Top 40 dance remixes. By the far wall there are tables piled with buffet trays and a beautiful dessert cart. Pretty class act.

"Over here!"

We turn to see several very popular seniors beckoning us over to their table. At first I think they must be mistaking me for someone else, and then I remember I'm with Jake. And just 'cause he's been blinded by my Vampire Scent doesn't mean that he's suddenly lost all coolness points with the in crowd. Suddenly I feel much better. I, Sunshine McDonald, somewhat geeky sophomore, will be spending the evening with the A-list.

"Hi Jake, hi Sunny," the aforementioned A-list cries as we sit down at their table. Wow. They even know my name. How cool is that?

"Sunny, you look beautiful," says Rick, the captain of the football team, who sits to my left.

"Yes, you're like the most beautiful girl in Oakridge," agrees Sam, the basketball player across the table.

I can feel my face heat. Wow. These A-listers are so nice. So welcoming. So . . .

So pissing off their girlfriends.

Uh-oh.

I look around the table. All the guys are drooling and all the girls are giving me the most evil stares known to humankind. Crap. This Vampire Scent thing can really backfire if you're not careful. Free dresses from smitten clerks—good. Making the entire cheerleading squad want to kick your ass—very, very bad.

"Jake, let's dance," I say, even though we've just arrived and there's barely anyone on the dance floor. I mean, dancing before dinner? How uncool can you get? But I'm desperate to get away from this table before the girls go all Charlie's Angels on me.

Luckily Jake is, of course, still bewitched by me and will do anything I say, even if it's social suicide. So though I'm positive we look absolutely ridiculous all alone on the dance floor, he obeys my command. Even more luckily, Jake's still the most popular guy at Oakridge. So as soon as he gets up to dance, half the senior class follows suit.

Me. A trendsetter. I could get used to this.

The DJ throws on a slow song and Jake proceeds to pull me close. I nestle my cheek in his chest, enjoying the feel of his lanky, muscular body pressed against mine, his chest rising and falling with his breath.

Ah. This is nice. Normal high school stuff. Exactly what I've been craving.

Well, that and the pulsating vein on the side of Jake's neck. But I won't go there. I will not, under any circumstances, bite my prom date. At least not in public.

"You're so beautiful," Jake murmurs into my ear. "So, so beautiful. You've got me completely addicted."

Sigh. Great, here he goes again. I wish he'd just shut up. I mean, I like hearing that he thinks I'm beautiful, don't get me wrong. It's just that every time he says it, I'm painfully reminded of the fact that in real life he's, as the self-help book says, just not that into me. That, in reality, this is all an illusion that will end as soon as I drink the Grail blood and turn back into a pumpkin.

Cinderella, I feel for you, girl.

Whoa! My head spins as Jake suddenly decides to get creative on the dance floor. He dips me backward without any kind of warning. As I scramble to keep my balance, my eyes fall on a surprising prom guest.

Make that two very surprising prom guests.

I regain my balance and break away from Jake's embrace. "I'll be back," I tell him, patting him on the arm and trying to appear composed. "I just want to go say hi to someone."

Say "hi" or "what the hell do you think you're doing here and why did you bring him?" to be exact, but Jake doesn't need to know the sordid details of my upcoming convo.

"Hurry up, babe," he says, dipping his head to plant an unexpected, way-too-PDA kiss on my lips. "I'll miss you every second you are gone."

"Hurry. Right. Okay," I agree as I back away. Once I'm at a safe distance, I turn and make great strides to the punch bowl.

I'm going to kill her. I'm going to kill her. I'm going to kill her. I'd kill him, too, if he weren't already dead.

"What are you doing here?" I hiss at my sister, who's dressed (surprise, surprise) in a lacy black Gothic princess dress that's completely inappropriate for prom.

Rayne scowls. "Nice to see you, too, sis," she says.

"You're not a senior. You're not on the guest list."

"Really. Go figure. Maybe I—ohhh," she makes an overly dramatic shriek, "maybe I sneaked in." She fans her face with her hands. "Oh, shock, horror. Call the police. I broke into Oakridge's senior class prom. Past all the teachers and Homeland Security spies. All the way to the punchbowl. Watch out, senior class . . . there's an evil sophomore in your hotel."

I roll my eyes. "You're so not funny. And you still haven't answered my question."

"Which was?" Rayne asks sweetly.

I hate her. I absolutely hate her. Can you emancipate yourself from your twin sister? If so, I'm definitely filing the paperwork Monday morning.

"Why. Are. You. Here?" I ask, spelling it out slowly, through clenched teeth. "And. Why. Did. You. Bring. Him?"

"Him?" Rayne asks in a ridiculously innocent voice. As if she hasn't a clue who I'm talking about. "Oh, you mean Magnus?" she concludes. "Well, I needed a date and he wasn't doing anything and . . ."

I squeeze my hands into fists, not quite convinced I shouldn't wind up and smack her. The proximity of the senior class advisor, Mr. Moody, is the only thing that's stopping me at the moment.

"This is *my* night," I growl at her. "*Mine*. I am on a date with the hottest guy from Oakridge High. And I refuse to let you spoil this for me."

"I'm not spoiling anything. We're just here to dance and drink punch."

"Yeah, right. I know you too well, sis," I spit out. My stomach is churning with fury. "You came to rub it in. To flaunt it in my face."

"Really, Sunny, you should work out these anger issues of yours," Rayne says with a *tsk-tsk*. "I have no idea what you're talking about, but you sound like you need some serious help." She grabs the ladle and pours herself a cup of punch. "Go back to your date and enjoy the prom. Magnus and I will stay out of your hair."

"Yes, don't worry, we'd never want to ruin your dream night," Magnus agrees, coming up from behind Rayne.

The second I lay eyes on him everything inside me starts doing crazy things all at once and I feel like I'm going to pass out. My hands start shaking. My stomach is nauseated. My heart aches. Tears form at the back of my eyes and I suddenly find it difficult to breathe.

He looks so good. Dressed to the nines in a dashing tux. He's chopped his long hair to ear length, long layers in the front hanging casually in his face. His amazing blue eyes look even bluer, if that's even possible. But the warmth I've found comfort in is long gone. Instead he gazes at me with an icy stare.

Gulp.

It takes everything inside me not to throw myself in his

arms and cry and cry and hope that he'll hold me and comfort me and tell me everything will be okay. But he won't tell me that this time. He'll shove me away and wrap his arm around Rayne's waist to show me that *she's* his new blood mate now. And later they'll go back to the coven and giggle at how ridiculous I acted at the prom and how clearly I'm still holding a torch for Magnus, even though I'm the one who technically broke up with him first.

I glance back at Jake. My dream date. He and his buddies are slapping each other on the back, having a grand old time. One guy passes around a silver flask filled with God knows what kind of alcohol and Jake takes a long swig. Then they giggle some more, evidently oh-so-pleased by their juvenile delinquency. I cringe, wondering what Magnus thinks of their immature behavior.

I suddenly feel very old and jaded.

I look back at Magnus and Rayne, blinking back tears. How could I have been so stupid? How could I have let Magnus go? He's everything I ever wanted in a boyfriend. He's sweet and loyal and nice and funny and oh-so-handsome. He did everything in his power to assist me on my quest to regain my humanity, even though it was against his best interests.

And I've been so ungrateful. In fact, I didn't even properly thank him for all he's done. I just said, "Thanks for the memories, dude," and ditched him like a bad habit as soon as I got what I wanted and he could no longer help me. I wouldn't even agree to meet up with him tonight, for a proper good-bye.

I am the biggest loser on the planet. I don't deserve him. In fact, I don't deserve anyone. I deserve to be an old maid, living all alone, with fifty cats to take care of.

I steal another look at Magnus and suddenly all the stupid excuses I've been making about why it'd never work out between us seem ridiculous and naive. And suddenly all the reasons I've wanted to stay human seem inconsequential.

I want to be with Magnus. No matter what I have to give up.

It'd be worth everything.

Even my soul.

But it's too late.

Isn't it?

Rayne looks from Magnus to me and back to Magnus again, her expression unreadable.

"I've got to pee," she suddenly announces, without ceremony. And before I can say, "Do what you have to do," she's already gone.

Leaving me alone with Magnus.

Was this her plan all along? Could my evil boyfriend-stealing twin actually be a saint in disguise?

I wonder . . .

I stare at Magnus. He stares back at me. You could cut the tension in the room with a knife. I realize it's up to me to make the first move. I was the rejecter in this whole mess. He opened himself up to me. Told me how he felt. And I threw it all back in his face. I am the one who needs to make serious amends.

And I'm ready to do so now.

"Magnus, I'm—"

"Sunny, there you are!" Before I can protest, arms wrap around my waist from behind. I whirl around. Jake grins at me, looking like a lost, slightly drunk puppy dog.

I look back at Magnus, who is watching the scene with cool eyes. This is not good.

"I've been looking everywhere for you, my love," Jake says, squeezing me tight. *Gah! Go away, dude! You're screwing up everything.*

But Jake doesn't go away. Instead he leans into me and starts messily kissing my neck. "Oh God, I love you so much, Sunny," he murmurs too loudly. Way too loudly.

Magnus's eyes narrow. "I've got to get going," he mumbles.

"No Mag, wait!" I cry. But he's already halfway out of the room. Vampires can really move when they want to.

I've got to reach him. To tell him how I feel before it's too late!

"I beg of you, Sunny, my love, please never leave me!"

"Oh, eff off, Jake!" I cry, while squirming to get away. I know full well I'm damning my one and only chance to be A-list in high school. To date a Sex God and be the envy of all my friends. But I totally don't care. In fact, I don't care if I turn into the biggest social reject Oakridge High has ever seen.

As long as I get to talk to Magnus.

But Jake isn't letting go without a fight, so I give him a little persuasion.

In other words, I stamp on his foot. Hard.

With spiky heels.

And vampire strength.

He lets go, yelping in pain. I hope I haven't put an actual hole in his foot. Oh well, no time to check now.

I sprint to the ballroom exit. This is like Cinderella in reverse, though I'm sure Magnus isn't going to leave a glass slipper behind. Maybe a Prada loafer . . . ?

I'm outside before I catch up to him. He's walking through the parking lot, his head bowed and his steps slow. He looks like he's lost his best friend.

What he doesn't know is that his best friend wants him back. Badly.

"Magnus!" I cry.

He stops in his tracks, not turning around. I rush over to him, grab his hands. I'm so out of breath it isn't even funny. I really need to clock in some quality time at the gym when all this is over.

"Magnus," I repeat, panting. We lock eyes. His look so sad, it breaks my heart. "I'm sorry. I didn't mean—"

"Sunny, I—" he says.

And suddenly we're talking and crying and laughing all at the same time. Apologizing, explaining, begging for forgiveness.

"I love you, Magnus," I say after we both pause for breath. "I didn't realize it. Or maybe I did, but I didn't want it to be true. I thought it would be way too complicated. And I was too concerned with being normal. But I don't care anymore. I love you. And I want to be with you. Forever. No matter what it takes."

"I love you, too, Sunny," he says, reaching over and brushing a bloody tear from my eye. "Accidentally biting you was the best mistake I've ever made in my life."

Aw. He's so sweet. So wonderful. So—

So kissing me.

Our mouths clumsily find one another, desperately seeking everything from the other person. Seeking and finding, I might add. Finding acceptance. Desire. Love. The works.

It's so wonderful I can barely stand it. He loves me. Magnus loves me. It's unbelievable for me to even comprehend how great that is.

As we kiss, his arms wrap around me and pull me close to him. We fit perfectly together. Like we were made for one another. And maybe we were. After all, I know we have compatible DNA.

I honestly wouldn't mind kissing him all night. Never going back into the prom. Never having to face my crazy, obsessed date. Make this my new reality and forget everything about the world. If I had Magnus at my side, I'm sure I could do it in style.

Then Magnus pulls away, glancing at his watch. At first I'm irritated. Like, hello? Does he have somewhere he needs to be or something?

"It's almost time," he says.

I cock my head in confusion. "Time? For what?"

"For you to drink the Grail blood."

"But . . ." I scrunch my eyes. "I'm not . . ." Didn't he listen to a word I just said? I love him. I want to be with him. And that means giving up my humanity for him, obviously. Doesn't he want me to?

"Not?" His turn for the confused look.

"No, Magnus." I shake my head. "Don't you get it? I'm not going to drink it. I'm going to stay a vampire so I can be with you."

He frowns and takes my hands in his, bringing them up to his chest. I can't feel his heart beating, but that's probably only because he doesn't have one.

"No, Sunny," he says firmly.

"Huh? What do you mean, no?"

"I won't allow you to remain a vampire for my sake."

"But . . ." Doesn't he want to be with me? Or was this all some kind of sham? I can feel my heart tearing apart inside. "But I love you," I say, almost afraid to admit it again.

He smiles softly and leans forward to kiss me on the forehead. "I love you, too," he whispers. "That's why I can't allow you to remain a cursed creature of the night. I want you to have the gift of life I never had."

"But I thought you said you liked being a vampire."

"It has its moments," he says with a shrug. "But at the same time, it can be a lonely life. And forever is a long time to live." He pulls me tight into an embrace. "I don't want you to suffer like I have. I want you to be you. The human you that I love."

"But then, but then . . ." I can't seem to form a sentence. This is not going the way I had planned at all. Not that I had really planned it out, but if I had, this wouldn't be the scenario. In my planned version, he'd be thrilled that I wanted to stay a vampire. We'd crush the blood vial and retreat to his coven and be one with one another, forever.

That's it! That's what I need to do.

I pull out the vial from my purse and before I can have second thoughts, I slam it on the ground. Then I smash it with my foot. Blood and glass go flying, staining my once-adorable stilettos.

I swallow hard. There. It's done. Over. *Finito*. No turning back now.

I am a teenage vampire.

"Why did you do that?" Magnus cries, looking horrified.

"Because I want to be a vampire," I say stubbornly. Oh God, what have I done? What possessed me to do that? Panic sets in fast and furious.

"But you don't," Magnus insists, not making it any easier. Why can't he just be happy? Why can't he throw his arms around me and say he was hoping I'd do that? That I've made him the happiest vampire alive and he can't wait to spend eternity with me. Or do something besides stare at me with an incredulous look on his face, saying things like, "But you hate being a vampire."

"I've changed my mind," I say firmly. No need to show him my doubts and fears and overall freak-out. "I've grown to enjoy the whole vampire thing over the past few days. And I think it'd be a charming way to spend eternity."

"You're just saying that because you think that's what I want to hear," Magnus says, sighing deeply. "But you don't really mean it. Sunny, I know you too well."

Jeez. This is not turning out how I'd hoped it would. At all. Where are all the tender embraces? The taking me back to the coven and celebrating my new unlife?

"Well, what's done is done," I say, attempting a casual shrug. "No turning back now." I stare down at the Grail splatter on the pavement. I wonder if I got on my knees and licked . . .

No. That's ridiculous. It's gone. It's done. I'm a vampire and I'm more than thrilled about it.

"Do you want to go . . . inside?" Magnus asks abruptly. "Maybe dance or something?"

Dance? I stare at him in disbelief. How can he think of dancing at a time like this? I've just sacrificed my whole humanity and all he can think of is getting his groove on?

I shake my head, too depressed for words. "No, I'm good," I say, though, of course, I'm not really. Not really good at all, if you want to know the truth.

"Okay," he says. "Do you mind if I do? I have to . . . use the little vampire's room."

I smile halfheartedly. "I'll wait here."

I lean against a nearby car, watching him as he heads back inside. I love him. So, so much. I have no doubts about that. And I really do want to be with him forever. So why am I so depressed? I made my decision. There's no turning back now. Sure I sacrificed my humanity, but it was for the guy I loved. So totally worth it.

I'll probably learn to love being a vampire. I'll get assigned my own Donor Chicks. (Or maybe hot Donor Males, heh, heh!) I'll travel the world. Rule as queen by Magnus's side. We'll vanquish evil slayers, etc. Sounds like a blast. Much better than high school.

Of course transitioning is going to be a bit difficult. I can never tell my mom—she'd just lock me up in a place where doctors would stick tons of needles in me and do all sorts of crazy experiments like I'm some kind of lab rat. Ugh.

No, it'd be better if my mom thinks I'm dead. I'll fake a car crash or something. Those always seem to happen around prom time anyhow. Sure, she'll be sad at first. But then she'll eventually grow to accept life without her daughter. And anyhow, she'll still have Rayne. Well, until Rayne gets to the top of the waiting list again and becomes a vampire herself.

Sigh.

At least I'll get out of going to high school, I remember, brightening a bit. All those pop quizzes and complicated projects? Never again. Though I will miss performing the starring role in *Bye Bye Birdie*. Wow, my being dead is going to really screw up the play. As far as I know there's no understudy to the understudy. I may have inadvertently caused the whole school play and everyone's hard work to collapse. They'd totally kill me, if I weren't already pretending to be dead.

And then there's field hockey. But my teammates will be fine without me. Well at least against everyone but Salem. Salem's pretty tough.

And lastly there's Audrey. My best friend. She's going to be really shocked when she comes back from Disney World on Monday and finds out I've dropped out of school, field hockey, and drama. Oh, and that I'm dead, too, of course.

Wow. Who would have thought so many lives would change if I weren't around? Go figure. Nice of me to suddenly come to this realization after it's too late.

"Sunny, are you okay?"

I look up. Magnus has returned from his trip to the bathroom and is staring at me with a very concerned look on his face. At first I have no idea why, then I realize I'm crying. Stupid blood tears.

"I'm fine. Wonderful. Very happy," I say, swiping at my face. I don't want him to think I'm having second thoughts. Not that I am, really. At least not about him.

He closes the gap between us and takes my head in his hands. Running his fingers through my hair, he pulls me close and kisses me. Suddenly, I'm feeling much better. Concerns about school and parents and friends evaporate as I enjoy the sensation of his lips on mine.

I can do this. I can stay a vampire. Stay with Magnus. Be happy and live a fulfilling eternal life.

His kisses trail down my face to my neck. I love neck kissing. And being a vampire's girlfriend, I figure I'll get to experience a lot of it.

And then a searing pain shoots through my entire body.

"Ow!" I cry, pulling away. "Why the hell did you just bite me?"

28

Boys That Bite

I jump away, my hand to my neck like so much déjà vu.

"That hurt!" I cry. In fact, it hurt a lot worse than the first time he did it, a week ago at Club Fang. The Club Fang bite was just a pain in the neck, so to speak. This one feels like poison is shooting through every vein in my body—my head to my toes to my fingertips.

"Sunny, sit down." Magnus commands. Dazed and in massive pain, I allow him to drag me down to the curb. I struggle for breath.

"What did you do to me?" I cry. I feel like I'm dying. Not that I know what dying feels like, but I'm pretty sure this can't be far off on the pain scale. My head hurts. My body aches. I feel sick to my stomach. It's awful.

Magnus pulls out his implanted teeth and presents them to me. "I'm sorry, Sunny," he says solemnly. "I thought it was for the best."

"What was?" I sob, begging the pain to go away. My whole body is practically convulsing like I'm having a seizure. "Did you poison me?"

He sighs and opens his other hand. I stare at it, then up at him.

The other Grail vial.

And it's empty.

I put two and two together.

"I'm sorry, Sunny," Magnus says. "I know you say you want to be a vampire, but honestly I don't believe you. In fact, I'm willing to bet a gallon of blood you're just saying that because you want to be with me."

I hang my head in shame. The physical pain has subsided somewhat, but the mental anguish is just beginning. What can I say? Of course, he's right. But I don't want him to think that's any reflection on my feelings for him.

"So I guess it wasn't meant to be," I say with a sigh. Great. Now I'm happy to be turning back into a human, but depressed as all hell about losing Magnus.

"What wasn't?" Magnus asks gently.

I look up in surprise. "You and I. Together."

He smiles that signature sweet smile of his and takes my hand. I tremble as he strokes my palm.

"Are you kidding?" he asks. "Vampire or human or, hell, if you decide one day you're going to become a werewolf or elf, I'm not letting you go."

For a moment I'm tempted to ask if there really are werewolves and elves out there as well as vampires, but then the full impact of his words hits me.

"Really?" I ask, choking out the words through my happy tears. "You want to be with me anyway? Even if I'm not your blood mate?"

He nods. His eyes are full of love.

"But it'll be hard to . . ."

"We'll make it work."

"And what if you get assigned . . . ?"

"You don't have to worry.

"But what if the other vamps—"

"I'll take care of them." Magnus places a finger to my lips. "The lady doth protest too much," he quotes.

I grin sheepishly. "You just met me?"

He laughs, then his face turns serious.

"Sunny, I love you. No matter what. We will make things work. I have full confidence in our relationship." He pauses, then adds, "You may not be my blood mate, but you certainly are my soul mate."

Aw. In fact, major aw-age. I love him so much.

Then, before I can come up with something equally endearing to respond with, he kisses me. A lot. I'd give you details, but I figure it'd just be way TMI and really, who wants that? Plus, a girl has to have some secrets, right?

Just suffice it to say, I happily kiss him back.

Human to vampire. Vampire to human.

Hey, it works for us.

Epilogue

Blog Entry 407
Author: Rayne McDonald

So there you have it. My sister, Sunny, is officially a member of the human race again. (And yes, her freckles are back, nyah-nyah!) She and Magnus (who was really never my type anyhow! I need someone wayyyy more dark and brooding) are officially an item. Boyfriend and girlfriend. Vampire and human. Doesn't matter, they're nauseatingly happy together. And Magnus has installed himself as official Master of the Blood Coven, Eastern U.S. region. All's well that ends well, right?

Well, not so much.

To make a long story short, here I am walking through the hallways of Oakridge on the Monday after the prom, feeling pretty good about myself. Giving the finger to various meathead jocks, avoiding the teachers who want to put me in detention for skipping class to go smoke over at "The Block," flirting with the new kid who's wearing an Interpol shirt. (He's not that cute, but evidently has good taste in music.) You know, your typical Rayney day.

Suddenly, out of nowhere, some old guy grabs my arm and starts dragging me into a side corridor. "You must come with me," he says in an urgent voice.

I'm just about ready to go tae kwon do on his ass, but then I realize it's Mr. Teifert, Sunny's drama coach.

"Dude, I think you've mistaken me for my twin," I say, as he drags me down into the auditorium's backstage area. "I'm Rayne. Sunny's the one in your play, not me."

The teacher pulls on the door and slams it closed with a loud ominous clanking sound. Hmm, cool sound effect. I could use that in my film. (Did Sunny tell you I'm a budding filmmaker? I'm going to be the next Tim Burton or David Lynch, just FYI.)

"I know who you are, Rayne," Mr. Teifert says, scratching his balding head.

I raise an eyebrow. "Oh. Then maybe an explanation of why you dragged me in here might be in order, don't you think?"

He nods. "Yes, yes, of course." He takes a deep breath. "Now brace yourself. This may be a little difficult to take in at first . . ."

Um, he isn't going to tell me he's in love with me, is he?

That would be extremely gross. I mean, sure, I dated my English teacher for two weeks last semester, but he was a sexy twenty-two-year-old Australian who liked Nietzsche. Mr. Teifert's practically ancient—at least forty, I'd say—and so not sexy or cute or Australian. Besides, once I caught him singing show tunes, so I'd been thinking he might bat for the other team.

"What I'm going to tell you may come as a bit of a shock," he continues in an extremely serious tone.

Jeez, enough with the drama, drama-teacher guy.

"Shock. Awe. I gotcha. Spit it out." After all, I'm late for class. Not that this would normally bother me.

He clears his throat. "Very well then. Once a generation a girl is born who is destined to slay the vampires."

I stare at him. "You know about Bertha?" I ask incredulously. "You know about vampires?" Okay, he's right. I am shocked. And awed. And all that. I had no idea this geeky old balding teacher had any clue about the Otherworld. I guess that's why he acted so weird when Sunny and I were joking around in the auditorium last week.

"Bertha, um, has had some blood pressure problems," he stammers. "She's temporarily retired from the slaying biz."

"I see . . ." I say slowly. Too much drive-through super sizing for Bertha between slays, I guess.

"No, I don't think you do," Mr. Teifert says. "What I'm trying to tell you, Ms. McDonald, is that you are next in line."

"Next in line?" I swallow hard, not liking where this is going. "Next in line for what, exactly?"

Mr. Teifert smiles and holds out his hand. "Congratulations, Rayne McDonald. You are the chosen one. Slayer Inc.'s new official Vampire Slayer."

To be continued . . .

Join the Blood Coven!

Do you want . . .

Eternal life?
Riches beyond your wildest dreams?
A hot Blood Mate to spend eternity with?

We're currently accepting applications for new Blood Coven Vampires. Sign up, take the online certification course, and get on the waiting list for your very own Blood Mate.

You'll also get to go behind the scenes, learn coven secrets, meet the vampires, watch exclusive videos, and get a sneak peek at what's coming up next for the Blood Coven Vampires.

Blood Coven Vampires

www.bloodcovenvampires.com

Check out all the Blood Coven Vampire titles!

Boys That Bite
Stake That
Girls That Growl

More Blood Coven Vampire action

Bad Blood

coming soon!